MW01134929

PROTECTING AN
AMERICAN RIVER

NANCY F. CASTALDO

books for a
better
earth
TM

holiday house • new york

A **Books for a Better Earth**™ Title
The Books for a Better Earth™ collection is designed to inspire young people to
become active, knowledgeable participants in caring for the planet they live on.
Focusing on solutions to climate change challenges and human environmental
impacts, the collection looks at how scientists, activists, and young leaders
are working to safeguard Earth's future.

Text and photographs except those noted in the picture credits copyright © 2025 by Nancy F. Castaldo
All Rights Reserved

HOLIDAY HOUSE is registered in the U.S. Patent and Trademark Office.
Printed and bound in December 2024 at C&C Offset, Shenzhen, China.
This book was printed on FSC®-certified text paper.
www.holidayhouse.com
First Edition
1 3 5 7 9 10 8 6 4 2

Library of Congress Cataloging-in-Publication Data

Names: Castaldo, Nancy F. (Nancy Fusco), 1962- author.
Title: Riverkeeper : protecting an American river / Nancy F. Castaldo.
Description: First edition. | New York : Holiday House Publishing, [2025]
Series: Books for a better earth | Includes bibliographical references
and index. | Audience: Ages 10 and up. | Audience: Grades 4-6.
Summary: "America's "first river," the Hudson, and the Riverkeepers who
protect it, offer insight into the history of environmental activism and
how individuals and communities can learn by example to protect
watersheds all over the globe"– Provided by publisher.
Identifiers: LCCN 2023023534 | ISBN 9780823453771 (hardcover)
Subjects: LCSH: Riverkeepers–Hudson River (N.Y. and N.J.)–Juvenile literature.
Water–Pollution–Hudson River (N.Y. and N.J.)–Juvenile literature. | Stream
conservation–Hudson River (N.Y. and N.J.)–Juvenile literature. | Environmental
protection–Hudson River (N.Y. and N.J.)–Juvenile literature. | Hudson River
(N.Y. and N.J.)–Environmental conditions–Juvenile literature.
Classification: LCC QH76.5.H83 C37 2024 | DDC
333.91/6216/097473–dc23/eng/20231027
LC record available at https://lccn.loc.gov/2023023534

ISBN: 978-0-8234-5377-1 (hardcover)

EU Authorized Representative: HackettFlynn Ltd, 36 Cloch Choirneal,
Balrothery, Co. Dublin, K32 C942, Ireland. EU@walkerpublishinggroup.com

**FRIENDS OF MY HEART, LOVERS OF NATURE'S WORKS,
LET ME TRANSPORT YOU TO THOSE WILD, BLUE MOUNTAINS
THAT REAR THEIR SUMMITS NEAR THE HUDSON'S WAVE.
–"THE WILD," THOMAS COLE**

"You could not step twice into the same river; for other waters are ever flowing on to you."

The Greek philosopher Heraclitus may have said these words many centuries ago, but you might have heard something similar in a Disney song. Indeed Heraclitus was right, the river is always changing and you'll never encounter the same water twice, but it is always the same river. If you put your foot into the Hudson River, take it out, and place it back in again, isn't it still the Hudson River? But the water is ever-changing, especially in a river that flows two ways. Think about the water that spills over your feet in a river. Where did that water come from, and can you ever touch that water again?

CONTENTS

The Hudson Highlands' dramatic mountains on either side of the Hudson River have inspired the ghost stories of Washington Irving and also played a crucial role in America's Revolutionary War.

"Tell me a story of the river and the valley and the streams and woodlands and wetlands, of the shellfish and finfish," wrote Thomas Berry in his book *The Dream of the Earth*. Well, I'm going to tell you that story, a story about my river: the Hudson. You might have a river near you that you call your own. It also has a story. This story, of the Hudson River, probably intertwines with yours because it's, as Berry says, "a story that brings together the human community with every living being in the valley."

Riverkeeper's office is in view of the Hudson River in Ossining, New York.

INTRODUCTION: A RIVER OF LIFE

Stretching outside Riverkeeper Tracy Brown's office window in Ossining, New York, is the Hudson River. In the case of the Hudson, *Riverkeeper* is both an occupation and an organization. And the *river* is cared for by both. Tracy leads the charge in the organization to call out polluters and monitor the health of the river year-round. Her efforts are joined by about sixty community scientists and thousands of volunteers, as well as Riverkeeper staff.

At the helm of the Riverkeeper organization's patrol boat is the captain, John Lipscomb, and his yellow Lab first mate, Batu.

It's late spring, and the ice that cracked and groaned all winter on the river's surface has melted. Its waters are now flowing freely from high in the Adirondack Mountains in northern New York State to New York City, where it meets the Atlantic Ocean. After Riverkeeper's patrol boat's winter maintenance in the Chesapeake Bay, Captain John is back patrolling the 315-mile (507-km) river in New York State and northern New Jersey.

The river is alive with life. Eagles swoop down from high branches all along the river with massive wings beating in the cool spring air. Like water skiers, they touch the water feetfirst. Their talons grab fish out of the strong river current. Then, they fly skyward again to their sturdy twigged nests, where young eaglets hungrily await their next meal.

Where the river meets the sea near the Statue of Liberty, tourists on the deck of a Hudson River tour boat spot a humpback whale's tail rising above the surface as if to wave at those on the deck. Below the surface,

Everyone, young and old, enjoys the Hudson River.

the whale's enormous mouth is hungrily filling with fish called Atlantic menhaden.

Residents of towns and cities are busy all along the river. Children play in parks like Little Island in New York City while their parents chat and have coffee. People north of New York City scramble to catch trains roaring along riverside rails to and from work. Boats and barges glide past, including Riverkeeper's patrol boat that's as much at home on the Hudson River water as the eagles grabbing a meal and the whales swimming below.

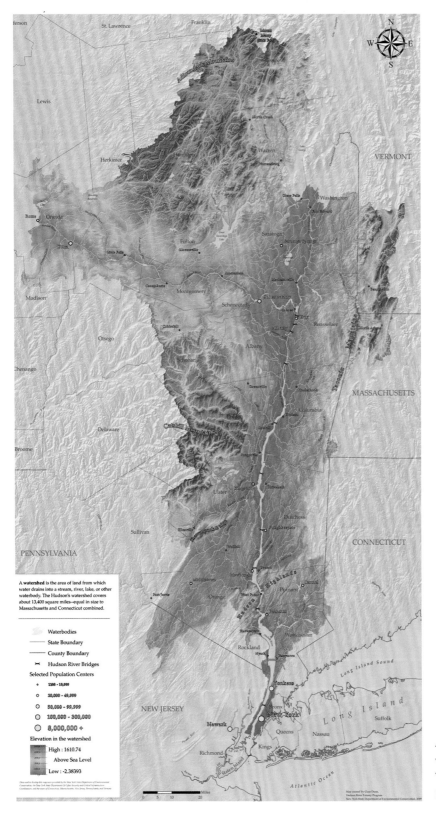

A map of the Hudson watershed from the New York State Department of Environmental Conservation

The Hudson-Athens Lighthouse has been guiding boats safely on the river's Middle Ground Flats since 1874. It is one of dozens that were built on the river and one of only seven that remain.

HUDSON RIVER STATS

Length: 315 miles (507 km)

Major Tributaries: The Mohawk River and Rondout Creek

Watershed Dams: At least 1,600

Cities Served by the River: Albany, Utica, Glens Falls, Troy, Poughkeepsie, Kingston, Yonkers, Beacon, Newburgh, Peekskill, New York City, and Jersey City, NJ

Towns Served by the River: Hudson, Athens, Coxsackie, Nyack, Piermont, Tarrytown, Sleepy Hollow, Cold Spring, Hyde Park, Rhinebeck, Tivoli, Cornwall-on-Hudson

Watershed: 13,344 square miles (34,561 sq. km)

Bridges: 7

Lighthouses: 7

1

THE RIVER

Some rivers, such as the Colorado River, flow from the mountains, run fast, and carve canyons. Others, such as the old Mississippi, flow slowly. Some, such as the Snake River, twist and turn through the landscape. Many flow like ribbons of water year-round, while others become dry. Every river is different, just like people. And each one is important.

Rivers provide us with fresh water for drinking and growing crops. They give us a pathway for transportation and recreation. In addition, rivers can provide a rich bounty of food for humans and wildlife. Rivers inspire us. The majestic Hudson River does all of those things. And like other rivers, it needs people to protect it, to keep it clean, and to ensure its *ecosystem* is healthy. The Hudson Riverkeeper plays a massive role in all three. And Hudson's Riverkeeper has forged a strong model for many other rivers, such as the Klamath River running through California and Oregon, that now have their own Riverkeepers and Waterkeepers to watch out for their health. After all, rivers provide life to us all. To examine how a Riverkeeper works, let's first explore the place where all rivers begin.

The Middle Ground Flats was once a sandbar, but the Army Corps of Engineers turned it into an island when it dumped dredge soils on it.

THE RIVER'S BIRTHPLACE

The starting place or source for a river is known as its *headwaters*. That special birthplace could be a spring, lake, or even a spot where smaller streams join together. The headwaters supply food and nutrients to the river, which in turn supports the health of the river community or ecosystem.

The Hudson River's headwaters are high up in the Adirondack Mountains of New York State. From a small body of water called Lake Tear of the Clouds atop Mount Marcy, the river's waters flow south for 315 miles, in rushing rapids and over boulders. The river becomes larger and mightier as other waters, called *tributaries*, join in on their way to the Atlantic Ocean.

For about half of its length, from New York City Harbor to the city of Troy, the river is a tidal *estuary* that ebbs and flows with the ocean tides. That means it has a mixture of salty and fresh water, called *brackish*. The salt water flows into the Hudson River during each high tide. The river's fresh water, at the same time, flows from north to south toward the sea. River tributaries also feed the river with fresh water. The *salt line*, the border of brackish and fresh water, can reach from the ocean up to the wide Tappan Zee Bay near the towns of Tarrytown and Nyack in the spring. It reaches north to the Newburgh Bay in summer and even farther north during droughts. This unique characteristic makes the river a vibrant ecosystem that teems with various aquatic life, including many fish, such as herring, that use the river for spawning and as a nursery habitat but spend most of their lives in the ocean.

While the headwaters are essential, there is another important place that determines the health of a river. It is the land through and under which rain and melted snow flows on the way to the river. That location is called the river's *watershed*.

The headwaters of the Hudson at Tahawus, NY, were once the site of mines, mills, and a bustling 1800s community.

If you looked at a topographical map that didn't show any country or state borders and only showed mountains, lakes, and rivers, you would view the world differently. You would see how rivers shape the landscape by tearing away rocks and soil to carve canyons. You would also see how rivers nourish the land areas with rich, fertile soil on their floodplains. All the land that surrounds those waterways is the watershed of the river. And that watershed might be part of a larger river's watershed. Eventually the water of the larger river makes its way into the ocean. A *water basin* is a larger watershed that is made up of smaller watersheds. New York State has seventeen major water basins, including the Lower Hudson River and the Upper Hudson River.

Protecting the watershed is vital to ensuring the ecosystem remains healthy and the river remains clean. We all live in a watershed of one river or another. Where does the water drain from your home? Some long rivers, like the Mississippi River, have watershed regions that cover millions of square miles and multiple states. Although the Hudson River watershed is considerably smaller, at more than 13,000 square miles (33,670 sq. km), the river has strongly impacted all other rivers as the first river in the United States to have a Riverkeeper. It now serves as a model for hundreds of Riverkeeper and Waterkeeper organizations throughout North America and the world. That legacy is crucial to our health and the health of our environment, but the Hudson River's history also had a huge impact on the country, even before it had a Riverkeeper.

THE HUDSON'S HISTORY

A river's natural history blends with its human history. While rivers are important to our lives, humans have a profound impact on rivers, too. For centuries humans have found that the richness of the Hudson River and its valleyhave made for easy living. Early Indigenous peoples, from the Munsee of the Lower Hudson Valley (also known as Lenape) to the Mohicans

About ten miles north of New York City, the Hudson River stretches about three miles across at the Tappan Zee Bay where one of the seven remaining Hudson lighthouses helps sailors.

and Mohawks of the Upper Hudson Valley, fished for striped bass in the spring and used the river for deer hunting. They called it Muh-he-kun-ne-tuk because, unlike many other rivers, the river is tidal. It flows two ways.

The river was a primary route of travel. In 1609 Henry Hudson, an Englishman, was hired by the British Moscovy Company to find a trade route to the Pacific Ocean. He sailed his ship, the *Halfmoon*, up the river. His travels encouraged other Europeans to come to the river valley. Those Europeans later renamed it the Hudson River after the explorer. The Algonquins brought beaver skins to trade with the new-comers, which became an invaluable trading resource that changed the history of New York and the country for the next two hundred years. Because of the Hudson and other navigable rivers in New York State, then called

The Lenape were the original inhabitants of Manhattan Island. This depiction, "Manhattan Island in the Sixteenth Century," memorializing the island before Europeans, was created in 1892.

New Netherland, a major fur-trading center developed. Cities sprang up.

Trade wasn't the only reason for travel on the river. The Hudson became a critical military route during the fight for America's independence from England. In an effort to stop British ships from sailing northward, a log boom affixed with a huge iron chain was successfully installed in May 1775 across the river in the Hudson Highlands, between revolutionary battlements. The blockade, along with cannon fire, prevented King George from cutting the New England colonies off. The geography of the mountains flanking the Hudson's shores in the Hudson Highlands proved a strategic advantage for American troops.

Hendrick (Henry) Hudson's voyages on the *Halve Maen* (*Halfmoon*) in the 1600s opened up the river to European development.

After the American Revolutionary War, the Hudson Valley settlement grew. Towns and cities formed and grew larger on the riverbanks. Brickmaking and ice-cutting were profitable. Farms were cut out of the forests, leading to the shifting sandbars in the river and silty waters.

Africans were forcibly brought here and enslaved to work in often brutal conditions with no compensation in early riverside industries. Slavery wasn't abolished until 1827 in New York State, and the last enslaved people in New Jersey weren't freed until 1866. Their skill and hard labor helped transform the Hudson into "America's First River."

The Hudson River's trade and travel route launched it as the most prominent and profitable waterway in America a century before the Mississippi Valley was settled.

The city of New York and the Hudson River Valley to the north continued to grow. The river valley attracted industry and workers. *Sloops* and schooners sailed north, transporting goods and people. Agriculture flourished. In 1825 the Erie Canal was completed, joining the Hudson River with Lake Erie. This new connection opened up three hundred fifty

Schooners like the *Apollonia* were a regular sight on the river when early European colonists sailed the waters.

more navigable miles for settlers, goods, and grain, leading to more development and linking New York and New Jersey to states farther west along the Great Lakes.

THE INDUSTRIAL REVOLUTION

Railroads came to the Hudson Valley in the 1800s, and industries sprang up alongside the river. But, despite the railroads, the river was still a major mode of transportation. It even served as a lifeline for many enslaved people using the Underground Railroad to gain their freedom.

New York City's population increased, and with that growth came the need for stone for buildings and roads. Attention turned to the Hudson's nearby cliffs known as the Palisades, where for several years the towering rocky borders of the Lower Hudson were blasted so that the stone could be used to construct the city's streets and skyscrapers. In the 1890s a group of women, including Mary Proctor and Edith Gifford, worked to stop the devastation of the majestic cliffs. Mrs. Gifford, a self-taught forestry expert, recognized the value of the old-growth forests of the Palisades as she saw them from the deck of the *Marietta* sailing on the river. As fellow passenger Mary Proctor later claimed, paving stones can come from anywhere, but the Palisades were unique. Their early preservation efforts of the Palisades would lead the way for others to protect the Hudson River *bioregion* years later.

Industry continued to grow in the 1900s, damaging the river ecosystem. Power companies that used the water for cooling would draw cold water out of the river and release warm water back into it, harming fish populations. Automobile manufacturers released polluting chemicals with paint residues. Other factories released harmful compounds, such as *PCBs* (polychlorinated biphenyls), into the waters. Even farms became polluters when toxic agricultural runoff washed into the tributaries and added nitrates and chemical pesticides, such as DDT (dichlorodiphenyl-trichloroethane), to the river ecosystem. Look back at that geographical map of the landscape. See the small brooks in the watershed that connect to rivers and the rivers that flow into lakes? They are all fed by *precipitation* and underground springs that can be impacted by *pollution*. And residents added trash and sewage to the river. All of this industrial and population growth helped the area to prosper economically but greatly endangered the river's health.

The threatened river drew interest beyond the activists who saved the Palisades. The threats to the river became widely known and had been

The cliffs known as the Palisades rising up on the New Jersey side of the Hudson in this early print inspired the first protections of the Hudson River.

written about for decades, including in Jane Jacobs's 1961 landmark book *The Death and Life of Great American Cities*. Jacobs wrote, "... up the Hudson River, north of New York City is a state park at Croton Point, a place for picnicking, ballplaying and looking at the lordly (polluted) Hudson."

WHY CAN'T WE SWIM OR FISH?

After centuries of exploiting the river for transportation and industry, the river became polluted. Adding to that pollution were the residents themselves. Trash and sewage poured into the waters from the villages and towns built up on the banks. By the mid-1900s, residents were asking, Can we swim or fish? The pollution caused many mid-twentieth-century parents to forbid their children to play in the waters. Teens in North Rockland, living across the river from the Indian Point Nuclear Power Plant in the 1970s, joked that swimming in the Hudson would make them glow in the dark from the pollution. What was the state of the water? Well, that depended on where you were on the river. Residents in some areas found dead fish on their shores, while Tarrytown residents were concerned with paint in the waters coming from the General Motors Corporation plant. But residents didn't know where or if it was healthy to swim, fish, or use the river for anything. Who could answer these questions?

SAVING THE RIVER

When the conservation movement was growing in 1960s America, a man spoke up on behalf of the river. Robert Boyle, a sportswriter and avid angler, wrote a book about New York State's Hudson River. He described the need for someone to work on behalf of the river, sort of a guardian or advocate. Boyle called this person a Riverkeeper. He founded the Hudson

River Fisherman's Association in 1966 to help protect the river by building cases against industrial polluters. For more than thirty years, the association worked on behalf of the river.

Boyle again used his voice in 1970. This time he wrote an article to alert the public to the problem of PCBs and other contaminants in the Hudson and other waterways. The Hudson River isn't the only river plagued by a mixture of dangerous compounds known as PCBs. First made by Monsanto Company in 1929, PCBs were released into rivers years ago by corporations that used them as coolants and lubricants in transformers, capacitors, and other electrical equipment. PCBs don't burn easily, so they functioned as good insulators, but they were also highly toxic.

In the October 26, 1970, issue of *Sports Illustrated*, among the basketball stories was Boyle's article titled "Poison Roams Our Coastal Seas." He wrote, "Coastal waters are infested with pesticides, metals and other toxic pollutants, and these poisons can kill fish, their young and the organisms they feed on." He continued to bring the message home to his readers: "It is also possible that this pollution, unless checked, may kill people." He called out high levels of toxins, including DDT pesticide residues, PCBs, and mercury in many spots, including the Hudson River. He made a difference. But he wasn't the only voice to lead the charge.

PCBS

Boyle's article was a stark warning that helped end the production of these compounds a few years later in 1977. Further scientific evidence showed that PCBs don't break down in the environment and can cause health problems. Unfortunately, they were used by many corporations, including General Electric (GE), and released into the river beginning in 1947. That ended in 1977 when Monsanto stopped production.

PCBs released into a river become part of the river's food chain. Tiny

Many people impacted the conservation of the Hudson River, including these two men. Arthur Glowka (left) helped found the Hudson River Fisherman's Association, Riverkeeper's predecessor, along with Robert H. Boyle (right).

organisms take them up and are then consumed by larger organisms. Along the way, the chemicals build up in the food chain. Ultimately the entire ecosystem, from fish to birds to humans, is impacted. PCBs are difficult to remove without dredging the river bottoms where they settle. After years of debate, the U.S. Environmental Protection Agency (EPA) and GE began the long cleanup by dredging PCB hot spots in the river. The cleanup and debate continues.

A DIRTY RIVER

"*Sailing down my dirty stream/Still I love it, and I'll keep the dream/That someday, though maybe not this year/My Hudson River will once again run clear . . .*" sang famous folk singer Pete Seeger in his song "My Dirty Stream" for his 1982 album *God Bless the Grass*. That song became a powerful anthem, the first of many Seeger wrote. But Seeger wasn't just a folk singer. He was an activist, bound and determined to bring awareness of the Hudson River's pollution to inspire its preservation. After reading the 1908 book *The Sloops of the Hudson*, he decided in 1966 to try to save the river with a sloop. The sloop would show people the pollution and, hopefully, shock them into action. So he launched a 106-foot-long Hudson River sloop in 1969, just like the ones that had sailed years before. It was named *Clearwater*.

On April 14, 1970, *Clearwater* sailed from New York City to Washington, DC, to join in the first Earth Day celebrations. Decades later, it still sails upon the river, conducting science-based environmental education programs and introducing the public to the river's challenges. As a result, the sloop is considered America's Environmental Flagship and was named to the National Register of Historic Places in 2004.

The public became more and more aware of the health of the Hudson. The first Earth Day, April 22, 1970, inspired more activism and protests about the Hudson's pollution, including *Clearwater*'s first sailing. Groups of demonstrators highlighted Con Edison's connection to the numbers of diseased fish from the river with a display of dead fish on Fifth Avenue in New York City. Demonstrations and calls for action continued for the following decade.

In 1983 John Cronin, a professional angler and congressional aide, was hired to patrol the Hudson full-time. The Riverkeeper program was officially born. The Hudson River was not alone in its problems. Rivers across the country experienced pollution. In fact, sometimes the pollution caught fire and rivers were seen with flames on the surface of their waters. The Riverkeeper program spread to communities that also wanted to clean and protect their rivers. It now continues throughout the United States and the world with more than three hundred fifty

The *Clearwater* sloop has been raising awareness for the river and educating people for decades.

The first woman at the helm of Riverkeeper since it formed about a half century ago, Tracy Brown, notes that most water protectors in traditional cultures are women.

organizations and partnering groups protecting more than 2.7 million square miles of waterways on six continents. Those Riverkeepers and Waterkeepers come from all different backgrounds.

THE BIRTH OF RIVERKEEPER

Tracy Brown is an environmental advocate and the first woman in the Riverkeeper organization's fifty-year history to hold the title of Hudson River Riverkeeper and president of the organization. Her job is to lead the charge as the organization tackles the challenges of protecting the Hudson River now and in the future and advancing the fight for "clean renewable energy and sustainable, nature-based infrastructure." According to riverkeeper.org, the term *nature-based infrastructure* describes ways that flooding, erosion, and runoff can be lessened using nature as a model. For example, planting trees will prevent riverbank erosion by holding the soil with their roots.

But Tracy doesn't do the job all by herself. She has many others who join her in the effort, including John Lipscomb, Riverkeeper's patrol boat captain. He has the critical job of physically patrolling the 5,000 nautical miles (9,260 km) of the river with his gallant first mate, a yellow Lab mix named Batu that serves as a companion and Riverkeeper ambassador.

Together they work to stop polluters, protect the river ecosystem, and safeguard drinking water for nine million people. The Riverkeeper team of volunteers and activists up and down the Hudson River Valley use science, art, activism, environmental justice, and other efforts to achieve the same goals.

In 2022 Riverkeeper marked the fiftieth anniversary of the Clean Water Act, a cause for celebration and the reason Riverkeeper can measure its success. The Clean Water Act set national goals of achieving "fishable, swimmable and drinkable" water for the country's rivers and lakes.

Riverkeeper gathers data by collecting water samples in the river and its tributaries to measure the act's "swimmable" goals. A water test can tell a lot about water quality. It doesn't just measure bacteria levels. Riverkeeper's river estuary samples provide lots of data for scientists. One sample can provide measurements for the amount of salt in the

Captain John Lipscomb is never without Batu on his Hudson River patrols.

water, known as *salinity* level. It can also measure the amount of oxygen, the temperature, and the amount of *chlorophyll*. Riverkeeper's large testing network also can give scientists a look at nutrient levels and detect any medicines that have found their way into the waterway. The organization's routine data collection doesn't go into the study of other toxic compounds, like PCBs, mercury, or heavy metals. Those are measured in other tests. They've found that about eighty percent of the samples collected meet the U.S. Environmental Protection Agency's criteria for safe swimming. Is eighty percent good enough? No, but that number is better than it was fifty years ago.

Tracy Brown and Riverkeeper look beyond the goals. They strive to keep the river vital for humans and wildlife. As Riverkeeper, she has added some goals of her own and takes the organization's value and impact personally. How does she do that? Let's see.

2

THE RIVERKEEPER

Tracy Brown stood in the sand at the Philipse Manor Beach Club while river water washed over her feet on a steamy July afternoon. The sounds from a few giggling children swimming and the whistles of osprey and blue-gray gnatcatchers were interrupted occasionally by the Amtrak train roaring through the nearby station just feet away. She was spending part of her workday holding meetings at the riverside park. What could be a better place for the Hudson River's Riverkeeper to work than a Hudson beach?

While Riverkeeper is a not-for-profit organization, which relies mainly on donations and grants, it is also the title of the person at its helm, Tracy Brown. All Riverkeepers, Tracy included, have taken many different paths before arriving at their positions. Some were river guides for rafting companies. Some were activists. Some were lawyers. Some were fishermen. Tracy's pathway had art, community organizing, storytelling, and science pit stops. All those stops and experiences helped her, and her fellow

Riverkeeper Tracy Brown was first inspired to become an activist here at Philipse Manor Beach Club.

Riverkeepers, build the skills needed to become the advocate she is today. These different experiences give Riverkeepers unique ways of approaching their jobs.

Regardless of the paths they've taken, all Riverkeepers, including Tracy, are passionate about the river in their charge. One crucial skill they share is the ability to seek out collaborations and rely on others for their talents and opinions. Tracy compares herself to an orchestra conductor, there to support a team of committed, specialized experts who create a fantastic symphony together.

BECOMING A RIVERKEEPER

Tracy's journey to protecting the Hudson began as a young mom looking for a home around the Hudson River community of Sleepy Hollow in 2003. A friend invited her to the Philipse Manor Beach Club, where she took a swim on the quiet sandy beach.

"I was eight months pregnant, with a toddler in tow," Tracy recalled. "I took a swim in the Hudson and called my husband to say, 'Guess where I am?' His reply was, 'Is that safe?'"

Was it? She didn't know. So she set out to examine the river's health for herself and her family. That research jump-started her career in environmental activism, specifically to protect our living waterways. First, she went house-hunting in the communities beside the Hudson, keeping in mind that she wanted to co-parent with the river from her new riverside home. She believed that the river would be as constant and as important to their new life in the riverside community as would a loving parent.

"There's nothing like working to protect the watershed that you live in, and the river that you swim in and paddle on and sail on, and that you raised your family enjoying. The Hudson River is really where my heart is," said Tracy. Tracy's research led to her work as a volunteer activist. She eventually took a job at Riverkeeper.

A SYMPHONY CONDUCTOR

Tracy spent five years at Riverkeeper as water quality advocate before taking on her current role. Not only is she the first woman to hold her position, she's also the first working mother to hold the office as Riverkeeper since the organization's founding a half century ago. But it is not unusual for a woman to be an advocate for a living waterway. The Native Americans, for example, believe that water is life and have had women in the roles of water protectors for millennia. Tracy shares

"Living waterways are such an important part of the future of life on our planet. It's such an intergenerational concern," says Tracy.

their passion and identifies with water as a life-giving resource. She finds that many people she connects with also care deeply about waterways. And many are coming to these water issues in addition to raising children.

"Living waterways are such an important part of the future of life on our planet. It's such an intergenerational concern." This perspective is one of the reasons she moved here.

"People really feel life when we are at waterways . . . a life-affirming energy from the water when we are around it," she said with her feet in the sand that hot afternoon. "And when you are at a dead waterway that is filled with pollution, you can feel that too . . . the lack of presence and the sadness that comes with that."

Tracy knows something about polluted waterways. In spreading the news about Riverkeeper's work during her first position there, the information centered around targeting and reducing pollution, specifically sewage infrastructure. People would always ask Tracy if they could swim in the water, and the answer wasn't always clear. At that time there were only a handful of legal beaches on 150 miles of river, but many people would swim in other areas. Testing the water was crucial to know the answer. A collaboration with water-testing scientists was necessary. It turned out that leaking sewage was a significant source of river pollution. Reducing it became Tracy's focus and passion. She knew that other states had Right to Know Laws that informed the public about pollution problems, and she could see that New York also needed one. So Tracy searched for lawmakers next to make her case. Their involvement was crucial. Her persistence helped in the passage of two critical pieces of legislation. The New York State Sewage Pollution Right to Know Law passed in 2012, and the 2017 New York State Clean Water Infrastructure Act provided grants to fund upgrades to sewage collection and treatment.

Those early successes as a river activist also brought public awareness to Hudson River Valley residents that their behavior and practices affected the health of the river and themselves. Much of the pollution was located close to shore, where sewage and waste entered the river. It wasn't flowing from big corporations or industries like many believed. It was flowing from community sewage systems. It mattered how residents and communities handled their waste. As Tracy learned, the water-testing reports held up a mirror to the residents of river communities. That data became a game changer. It became harder to shift all the blame to industry and corporations. Everyone was responsible. And that also meant that everyone could turn the problem around. Voting for lawmakers who could pass protective legislation became important.

VOICES LIFTED

Legislation can make a bioregion like the Hudson River Valley healthier for people and wildlife. New York's Sewage Pollution Right to Know Law requires the public to be notified through local news and the New York

State Department of Environmental Conservation (NYSDEC) website within four hours of any sewage discharge. The success of this legislative campaign might not have happened without the approximately twenty thousand letters and more than forty-three thousand signatures collected in support of its passage. And, of course, Tracy Brown's Riverkeeper input. When people speak up, they can make a difference.

CURRENT CHALLENGES

While pollution is still a priority, Tracy and the Riverkeeper organization are extending their efforts to search for answers about the well-being of the entire river ecosystem, from the health of the fish and birds to the water quality and the impact of climate change on the ecosystem. And the biggest challenges now stem from climate change. The warming of the planet and the rising sea levels impact the entire ecosystem. As a result, we see more storms and more flooding.

"Water is life-giving, but also life-taking," said Tracy.

Tracy and Riverkeeper must work hard to focus on river ecological restoration and preservation projects. Critical habitats like coastal marshlands and inland wetlands, must be protected and conserved. But it also means that Tracy and Riverkeeper have to continue doing what Riverkeeper has always been doing. They need to block further old, polluting energy installations and projects,

A new park is just one of the many accomplishments of Riverkeeper and other Hudson River organizations.

as well as hold the state and federal governments accountable for achieving lower greenhouse gas emission targets. They also need to ensure that the energy producers on the river and the energy delivered to Hudson Valley communities come from renewable sources.

A YEAR OF SUCCESSES

As Tracy Brown completed her first year as Riverkeeper, the organization celebrated victories, including its role in creating the Hudson Eagles State Recreation Area.

Unlike any other park on the Hudson River, the Hudson Eagles Recreation Area is located on a wild stretch of the river between Athens and Albany, where the river itself is the actual park. The twenty-six miles of river waters are a pearl in the state park necklace. It's named for the eagles that have made a tremendous recovery and call that area home. Once a population devastated by the pesticide DDT, eagles can now be spotted sitting on the river's winter ice, nesting in trees on its banks, and swooping down for a fish meal.

In addition to the park, Riverkeeper planted more than four hundred trees to restore healthy streams, helped to shut down one dangerous nuclear plant, and worked to enhance drinking water protections for twenty-three Hudson River communities. But that wasn't all.

Older efforts continued. Back in 2002, Riverkeeper discovered a Superfund-scale oil spill along Newtown Creek in New York City's Brooklyn borough. The patrol boat spotted a black, gooey substance in the water. A tremendous amount of Riverkeeper research led to the discovery of an underwater leak from an old oil installation on a property now owned by ExxonMobil. Riverkeeper did its homework. It sued ExxonMobil in partnership with the State of New York to force a cleanup.

Blue crabs are just one of the species of wildlife that has returned to brooks and streams after dams have been removed.

And because of the many additional sources of pollution into the *creek*, the U.S. Environmental Protection Agency declared the entire waterway a Superfund site. The Superfund classification launched the spill area onto a high-priority list for cleanup. That was a good thing. After years of work, the creek is better off, but the cleanup continues. Riverkeeper and partners, like the Newtown Creek Alliance, are now looking at the site for potential habitat restoration.

ON AND OFF THE RIVER

Protecting the Hudson River spreads out to safeguarding the river's watershed. It involves advocating for efforts to make the river cleaner and to ensure access for everyone. All communities deserve to be able to cool off on a hot day. But is the river's access public or private?

Riverkeeper strives to build partnerships and form collaborations to maintain access to all communities. It also gets involved in bringing resources to disadvantaged communities to stem pollution and protect residents. For example, Riverkeeper won a ban on using toxic coal tar in pavement products in New York State that put human and ecosystem health at risk.

Riverkeeper also works to have obsolete *dams* removed to restore habitats. In 2020, the organization facilitated the removal of three dams in the watershed. These had caused problems in habitats that are home to river herring and American eel populations. But prior to Riverkeeper removing a dam, agreements must be secured as well as funding for the project. In the past year, Riverkeeper also witnessed the return of freshwater life. Trout, eels, blue crabs, and others returned to the creeks of Quassaick Creek and Furnace Brook, where dams were removed. While Furnace Brook is the creek's colonial name, it was known to the Algonquins as Jamawissa Creek, meaning "place of small beaver." Riverkeeper prefers to call it by this name.

Like the dams on the Columbia River in the western United States that cut off migrating Chinook salmon, these dams had cut off river herring, eels, and other species from the river's estuary for centuries before their removal.

And there are small things that Riverkeeper does that hugely impact wildlife, such as advocating to help populations of striped bass by encouraging the use of circular hooks for catch-and-release fishing. This new requirement causes fewer injuries to fish and increases their survival rate after release.

Tracy wakes up in the morning and thinks, "How do I take this incredibly powerful resource that is the Riverkeeper team and help them go out and be as impactful as they can be?"

Before Riverkeeper can remove a dam, such as this one on Q Creek, agreements must be secured as well as funding for the project.

3
RIVERKEEPER ON PATROL

Captain John Lipscomb woke up at four thirty on a gray July morning to get ready to leave the Catskill dock and patrol northward to Waterford, New York. A light rain fell on quiet Hudson waters, and John felt the same excitement and energy he did every time he departed. "When I get to the boatyard, and I can get to go to the boat and my bud . . . and the motor starts, I still get a thrill out of departing," he said. "I'm genetically made to move with a boat. It's a lifetime of passage-making. I don't get on a boat to get there; I get on the boat to get on the boat. It's the travel that's the fun."

Captain John was underway by seven o'clock with his first mate Batu at his feet. Batu, known as @riverkeeperdog on Instagram, is a four-year-old yellow Lab mix that found his forever home on the Riverkeeper patrol boat, *R. Ian Fletcher*, with John. Not only does he keep John company, he also serves as a Riverkeeper ambassador at every port. That interaction is important for Riverkeeper and the entire Hudson Valley community. Batu is approachable and is definitely a conversation starter.

On this day they weren't alone. Researcher Carol Knudson from Lamont-Doherty Earth Observatory was aboard to collect water samples, which she's been working on for fifteen years. Carol has a degree in marine science and credits her years as a Girl Scout camper for making her interested in the environment. She claimed that spending two weeks away at camp was one of her greatest life lessons. Carol remembered the feeling of coming home after being away in the woods. "Feeling the walls around me . . . I didn't like that. . . . I wanted to be outside still. And that always made such an impact on me," said Carol. She sails with Captain John each summer.

There are seventy-four water-testing stations on the Hudson and its tributaries between New York Harbor and Waterford. John and

Captain John Lipscomb has been at the helm of Riverkeeper's patrol boat since 2000.

The Riverkeeper boat leaves a water-monitoring site and continues on to the next one.

Riverkeeper research partners, such as Carol from Lamont, have been sampling the water since 2008. They collect water samples each year from May through October. Samples were collected at a variety of river sites that include marinas, official and unofficial beaches that people use for swimming, at the mouths of tributaries that are flowing into the river, farther into the tributaries, and at spots in the very center of the river, where there is the least human impact. Those more remote points, such as the middle of Haverstraw Bay, provide a snapshot, said John, that is like "peeking through a window." It is like collecting a sample of ocean water from the middle of the ocean where humans have the least impact. All of those sites provide important data on the health of the river ecosystem and help answer the question of where and when we can swim safely.

That morning samples were taken at three sites in Catskill before leaving. They included the launch point but also the Catskill Creek river tributary.

SAMPLING THE WATER

John stopped the boat. Carol leaned over the side as Batu stood watch. To keep the water sample clean, she scooped up a container of water with gloved hands. Then she placed a black-and-white circular Secchi disk into the water to measure the river's clarity at that monitoring station. Sometimes you can look into a body of water and see all the way down to the bottom because the water is so clear. Other times you can't see even a foot below the surface. "It's a turbid river," said Carol. "There's lots of sediment." But, she added, clarity doesn't always reflect cleanliness. There are invisible pollutants that don't impact the water's clarity. In addition, the clearness or transparency can be affected by the number of algae present, pollution, or suspended *sediment* stirred up from the river bottom. But clarity is an important measurement to record at each site. It can indicate a change in the river. At the same time Carol collected her samples, a valve measured *pH*, *latitude*, *longitude*, salinity, *turbidity*, and percent saturation of oxygen in real time. Carol pressed a button at each water-monitoring station to log a data point to get that information at that site. That data can also be used with satellite imagery to see chlorophyll levels that might indicate *algal blooms*. All of this data helps Riverkeeper monitor the health of the river ecosystem.

The Secchi (sek-EE) disk was invented in 1865 by an astrophysicist, Father Pietro Angelo Secchi, who was a scientific adviser to the Vatican. It was used to measure the clarity of the Mediterranean Sea and is still used today.

Carol Knudson, a scientist from the Lamont-Doherty Earth Observatory, can flip back through data sheets to compare data collected over her fifteen years with Riverkeeper.

Carol Knudson places the Secchi disk ino the water to test the river's clarity.

Riverkeeper docked in Waterford on the fifth day of a fifteen-day patrol.

SAILING NORTH

John, Carol, and Batu sailed underneath the Rip Van Winkle Bridge by Catskill, past the homes of historic Hudson River landscape artists Frederic Church and Thomas Cole on opposite riverbanks, and past the Hudson-Athens lighthouse.

Captain John and Carol continued testing northbound river sites in Hudson, Athens, Coxsackie, Coeyman's Landing, Castleton-on-Hudson, Island Creek/Norman's Kill, Albany, Troy, and finally on to Waterford before John would continue alone for a few days to sample the Hudson's largest tributary, the Mohawk River. The rain continued on and off, and the boat sailed on. They arrived in Waterford in the early evening and put the samples in the incubator. After incubation, their composition is recorded to provide scientific data on the oxygen and bacteria levels of the water that Riverkeeper then records on its website. Changes in bacteria levels are examined, and everyone hopes the resulting data will reflect water safe for swimming. On this fifth day of his fifteen-day patrol, John also added the day's conditions in his logbook: light rain, thunderstorms, winds WSW (west/southwest).

Captain John has been at the wheel of the patrol boat since 2000. For more than two decades, the boat has logged more than eighty thousand miles. John has seen many sunny and stormy days over the years and has helped stop hundreds of polluters. In addition, he's also witnessed some pretty amazing things from his boat. He's seen the swoosh of silver herring fish leaping from the water in the river near Ossining. Near one of the river's navigation beacons, he's witnessed a returning family of osprey that seem to recognize Riverkeeper's boat as he sails by their nest each year. During this hot spell of summer weather, he spied one of the osprey parents with wings spread, shielding its young from the hot sun. That's something not many of us have the opportunity to encounter. But we must remember that most of what John encounters is below the water's surface.

UNDER THE SURFACE

Below the solid wooden hull of Riverkeeper's patrol boat lies a world inhabited by fish. There are herring, shad, and giant Atlantic sturgeon. Some of these fish can live for sixty years, grow to 14 feet (4.3 m), and weigh a whopping 800 pounds (363 kg). But that isn't all. There are also shellfish, such as crabs and oysters. And there are mammals, from enormous whales swimming around Manhattan Island to slippery river otters dipping beneath the water from the riverbanks. The tidal Hudson is unique. It has both brackish and freshwater wetlands. They act as critical, protective nurseries for many wildlife species, including striped bass, river herring, short-nose sturgeon, Atlantic sturgeon, shad, and eels that start their lives far away in an area of the Atlantic Ocean bordered by currents known as the Sargasso Sea. All these species are protected in the river's estuaries and tributaries, where they face fewer dangers as they mature than they would in the open ocean. The data that John and the others collect not only indicates the level of safety of the river for drinking and swimming, but also helps predict the health impacts of these species.

GIVING TRIBUTARIES BACK TO THE FISH

What keeps Captain John waking up each day to sail in all sorts of weather, from rainy days to sweltering heat? Despite all the marvelous things he's witnessed, there is weather to contend with and other frustrations. Water tests that don't improve and battles with corporations that the river and Riverkeeper don't win can add to the frustration level. In addition, days are often filled with more work than can be accomplished by nightfall. But what drives him on is that he knows that "any river, subject to human manipulation or impact, no matter how mighty, can't protect itself." His job is essential.

And then there are the wins, such as the historic 2016 undamming of the Wynants Kill Creek in Troy, that keep him motivated.

A WIN FOR WILDLIFE

The Wynants Kill was named after Dutch cabinet maker Wijnant Gerritsen van der Poel (1617–1699) who operated a sawmill. *Kill* is Dutch for "stream." The creeks and streams that connect to our rivers are known as tributaries. The 15.8-mile (24.4-km) Wynants Kill is a critical Hudson tributary.

These waterways act like a circulatory system in our landscape. Many of them have been dammed over the last two centuries to service our mills and industry. But these dams act as barriers to wildlife, such as herring that travel up the river to *spawn* in the tributaries. Dams also block the flow of nutrients and water to the area beneath the dam. Over the years dams become damaged, creating further disruption to the environment, with no one responsible for their upkeep. Riverkeeper works to remove the ones that are hazards and have outlived their usefulness to make the river ecosystem healthier.

Captain John spent fifteen years during his patrols learning how herring swim up the Hudson from the Atlantic Ocean to their ancestral breeding spot, but he knew something was blocking them from completing their journey. In 2013 he hiked up the creek and discovered a dam that he realized could be easily removed but had blocked the water flow for eighty-five years. Like many tributaries, the creek had been dammed for a mill, but that was over a century ago. The mill was long gone and the dam was uncared for and unneeded. If that wasn't enough, it was hindering the river ecosystem by cutting off a tributary for herring and other fish species.

There are two fish that are known as *river herring* in the Hudson River: alewife *(Alosa pseudoharengus)* and blueblack herring *(Alosa aestivalis)*. Just like sea turtles who return to the beach where they hatched and so many other wildlife species, these fish migrate to their ancestral waters to have their young.

Captain John says a 10-foot (3-meter) dam blocks fish as easily as a 500-foot (152-km) dam. These herring, like many of the Hudson's fish,

A crew dismantles the dam on Jamawissa Creek (also called the Furnace Brook).

were born in the Upper Hudson and its tributaries, where these waters act as a safe and healthy nursery for newly hatched herring. They were driven back by instinct to these rushing waters to spawn in the spring. This migration continued generation after generation. But as Captain John said, they'd "come up knocking at the door of that dam finding nobody home." Not only was it important for the fish species to enable them to spawn in the upper waters, but these fish were also crucial to the entire ecosystem. The tiny fish born in the upper waters would provide food for other wildlife, and the fish would help make the river rich with nutrients.

Riverkeeper, along with the City of Troy and the New York State Department of Environmental Conservation (NYSDEC), prompted the removal of the old, forgotten dam. "We're very proud of the City of Troy for being first in this initiative. By helping to restore life to this stream, Troy is demonstrating that communities can not only benefit from the river, they can also benefit the river in return," said Captain John. A camera was placed in the area when the dam was removed in May 2016. Just five days later, herring could be seen coming back. Again, thousands came back to the Wynants Kill, only this time they had a clear passage inland. The tributary was theirs again. John was thrilled. "It's a wondrous thing to be involved in something like that."

"Success is not just a fishable or swimmable river," said Captain John upon the dam's removal. "Now we want to restore the biological integrity to make it a living river again. That's the last step."

The dam in Troy was the first one in the history of the Hudson Valley to be removed expressly for fish passage, but it hasn't been the last. With the help of the New York State Department of Environmental Conservation, two more were removed to restore migratory fish passage. The century-old, hundred-foot-long, damaged Strooks Felt Dam on Newburgh's Quassaick Creek and Cortlandt's five-foot-high, seventy-five-foot-wide Furnace Brook dam in Cortlandt were removed in 2020.

DAM REMOVAL

It's not easy to remove a dam. Most company owners have long disappeared. Heavy equipment is required to dismantle the structure. Restoration is needed to repair the damage left by the heavy machinery.

Once the dam is removed, restoration begins, which includes plantings. Katie Leung is working on the banks of the stream.

But the removal can be life-changing for a river. It took more than a week to remove the small Strooks dam, which also involved regrading the streambed to stabilize the banks of the creek. There are more than one thousand, six hundred inventoried dams in the Hudson River estuary and watershed. There are probably a bunch more that are smaller and undocumented, too. These pose a threat to wildlife, but removing the obsolete ones will take money and effort. However, sooner or later, they all fall into disrepair. If the dams are not fixed, fish will eventually take over. Of course, from the standpoint of the fish, sooner is always better than later. That's where everyone who supports the river can step in—and not just on the Hudson. So many more obsolete dams around the United States and the world are waiting to be removed. Can wildlife wait until they are? We hope so.

BECOMING CAPTAIN

Everyone who works to protect and restore a river arrives a different way, and John's story is no different. Like so many others, John grew up alongside a river. In this case, his river was the Hudson. He remembers being held as he doggy-paddled above the river's sandy bottom. He day-dreamed in school while gazing out his classroom window at the river. His dad was a documentary filmmaker, and John learned a lot from him about caring for the environment. He also came to realize that the environment can often be an underdog. John grew to root for underdogs, especially the environment. He considers himself an "underdogist" and defines it as someone who becomes a champion, protector, or soldier for many nonliving and living things, such as the river. "The river is just waiting for us to do the right thing," he says, "and treat it well. It can't tell us [when it needs help]." John worked in the historic Petersen's Boat Yard in Upper Nyack, New York. Over the centuries the boat yard has built everything from schooners and steamers to boats for the U.S. Navy during World War II. John realized his passion for boats and the journeys they inspired.

He currently holds the position of patrol boat captain and vice president of advocacy at Riverkeeper. He's been working on behalf of the river for twenty-two years. Even though he's thought of slowing down, he keeps on going. "As you learn all about the river, it is hard to leave it," he says. He's had a lifetime of "passage-making" and claims that he doesn't go on the boat to get somewhere, but instead it's the journey, the travel, that he enjoys. That love continues with each voyage.

It's above 90 degrees Fahrenheit (32.2 degrees Celsius) as John settles in for the night at the Waterford dock. The hot night would make many question their decision to continue in this job, but John brings up another success. "The river can't say anything," he says, so the entire river community has to sometimes rise up to protect it. That happened in 2017, after the U.S. Coast Guard proposed creating ten anchorage sites on the Hudson River. The plan would have included spaces for up to forty-three barges to anchor in the river between Yonkers and Kingston. Everyone connected to the river, including Riverkeeper, could imagine the oil-laden tankers harming wildlife and negatively impacting the life of riverfront communities. It was time for everyone to spread the word and

Batu has a prime spot to see a perching osprey on the river journey.

lift their voices in opposition to protect the river. Thanks to Riverkeeper and others, ten thousand people raised their voices against the proposal. As a result, former New York governor Andrew Cuomo signed a bill in 2017 to safeguard the Hudson from the anchorage sites. Captain John and the Riverkeeper team cheered the victory. Another hurdle in river restoration was cleared, but they knew more would be ahead. Riverkeeper, its volunteers, partnerships, and collaborators would be ready to jump in.

4

IT TAKES A VILLAGE

While Tracy may be like an orchestra conductor and Captain John a crucial first chair, there are so many more who fill the seats in this river symphony. Some step into their seats for a short time, while others play year-round.

The cool, gray spring morning didn't deter more than a thousand volunteers who headed out to one hundred twenty-four Hudson River locations on May 7, 2022, for the Riverkeeper Sweep. This annual event drew volunteers of all ages, from kids to seniors, to the banks of the river from New York City northward to the Adirondack Mountains.

Riverkeeper's volunteer and outreach coordinator, Katie Leung, set out to partner with individual organizations and coalitions throughout the Valley for the annual cleanup day, called Sweep. She builds those partnerships and then supports them and their designated Sweep leaders with everything from help spreading the word to potential volunteers to obtaining permissions for dumpsters for the day of the event.

After working at the New York City Department of Parks and Recreation, Katie joined Riverkeeper in 2021. Although she loved her work documenting raptors in the city, Katie was drawn to the new

Riverkeeper's Katie Leung works to build community as she plans Sweep events with partner organizations throughout the Hudson Valley.

position because it would allow her the opportunity to engage more people in natural places. Working with existing Riverkeeper partners and establishing new ones seemed to her a Herculean task at first. Still, as she moved forward, she found it gratifying to see so many people wanting to be involved with the river.

THE HUDSON SWEEP

One partner for the damp spring Sweep that May was the Hudson Sloop Club. Club members and community volunteers met in the waterfront park beside the bustling train station in the town of Hudson, New York. Grabbing gloves, trash bags, rakes, and other implements, they headed out in search of trash on the park's riverbanks and then moved on to

A Sweep event with the Hudson Sloop Club volunteers gets underway.

the banks along the train tracks, where people often go fishing. It didn't take long for all the volunteers to start filling their bags and trucks with everything from bits of glass to cigarette butts to asphalt roofing shingles and even tires. There was even one spot that looked like a regular dumping site, and the group was able to fill the back of a pickup truck with numerous bags and a tire.

Fishers had left behind tangled fishing lines and bait containers. All of these items can harm wildlife and add to the river's pollution. Everything needed to be removed to protect the river community.

As Katie spent the day in her office, the command center for Sweep, volunteers were participating in Sweep events she had coordinated in other Hudson communities up and down the river. Some people volunteered at the Sweep for the first time, while many returned every year. All in all, everyone did their part to make the river cleaner.

Volunteers in Donahue Memorial Park in Cornwall-on-Hudson numbered seventy-five and collected 1,140 pounds (517 kg) of trash. They had the highest volunteer turnout; however, the Anchorage Marina in Eddyville proved to be the spot with the most trash collected— 2,820 pounds (1,279 kg)! This quantity of trash can seem overwhelming, but Sweep leaders at ten sites found their sites cleaner or improved from the previous years. That's good news!

WHAT DID THEY FIND?

These cleanups always bring in some surprising items. This year was no exception. Volunteers found buckets of tar, a smart tablet, a kayak, a box of 2011 SpongeBob SquarePants holiday ornaments, and enough shingles to cover a roof. In total, 18 tons of trash were removed, 1.3 tons of recycling, and 134 tires. That's super impressive, but that is just one year. Over the last eleven years, Sweep has hosted 1,068 projects, collected 322 tons of trash, and removed 1,810 tires from Hudson's riverbanks. The arm of Riverkeeper has also removed thousands of pounds of harmful invasive species and planted or maintained 6,025 native trees and plants. Those numbers are incredible! And as wonderful as they are, let's hope that one day the amount of trash cluttering the shoreline will decrease.

Other Sweep events throughout the year might help, according to Katie. While the public event occurs each May, corporations or individuals work with her to plan private mini events in the form of "One Bag Challenges" and custom Sweep events that serve as significant corporate team-building events and fundraisers for Riverkeeper. These

A Hudson Sloop Club volunteer picks up trash on the riverfront park's shore.

Sweep volunteers of all ages make a difference at the waterfront.

separate occasions help clean up trash throughout the year. They can also be planned by schools and scout groups.

Katie does other projects for community involvement. She helps set up Street Sweeps with volunteers in the cities of Hoboken, New Jersey, and Kingston, New York, to help clean up trash before it reaches the Hudson River and its tributaries. "We are trying to collect trash about three hundred meters away from the nearest body of water," said Katie. "In Kingston, that would be the Rondout Creek, and in Hoboken, it would be the Hudson." Along with the data gathered, engaging residents in these two underserved communities through Street Sweeps will instill deeper relationships between residents and their rivers.

Riverkeeper is also trying to promote a program to remove abandoned and derelict vessels. These are discarded boats left in the river or on its banks as trash. They are not only ugly to look at, but they also pose a hazard to wildlife and river navigation. Removing them is another step toward restoring the living river.

RIVERKEEPER'S HABITAT RESTORATION MANAGER, DR. GEORGE JACKMAN

Another crucial player in the Hudson symphony is Riverkeeper's habitat restoration manager, Dr. George Jackman. He worked in concert with Captain John to remove some of the small mill dams blocking the water pathway on so many of Hudson's tributaries. Dr. George is passionate about releasing these waterways back to wildlife.

Dr. George was elated to find so many species returning to the Jamawissa Creek near Cortlandt, New York, in Westchester County, after the dam removal project. Most of the excitement for everyone at Riverkeeper focused on the fish, but there was another aquatic species that caught Dr. George's attention—male blue crabs, known as *Jimmies*. According to Dr. George, Jimmies move into freshwater creeks for safety or cooler waters. The female blue crab is called a *Sally* and heads to more salty waters after breeding in brackish river water.

Some trash might seem unnoticeable or irrelevant, but even bits of glass need to be removed from the shoreline.

Volunteers collected fishing line left behind by fishers, which can tangle birds and other wildlife, and plastic bottles.

The Jimmies, however, reenter the freshwater creeks. Dr. George found Jimmies in both the Quassaick and Jamawissa Creeks upstream from the dam projects. In fact, he found the remains of one that had served as a meal for another wild species. That means that opening the creeks allows the crabs to enter the food chain there. That's important to the entire watershed. "We now consider blue crabs another migratory, *catadromous* species that benefits from dam removal," wrote Dr. George in an article. What an amazing discovery!

He calls these tributaries "umbilical cords between fragmented habitats" that provide life to these areas.

"There is an exuberant joy you feel when you see that thing demolishing that dam. It's a form of liberation. For me, it was like tearing down the Berlin Wall," said Dr. George. The dams block the water flow and create warming conditions that can lead to algal blooms.

According to Dr. George, the success of tributary dam removals has to do with serendipity. *Serendipity* is when something special and surprising is discovered. He and the Riverkeeper team, including Captain John, were trying to figure out all of the reasons why fish populations were drastically decreasing. As they set out to remove dams, they found some surprising results. They realized that once barriers were removed, "nature quickly heals the landscape's scars, free-flowing creeks more easily moderate flood waters, and the community of . . . aquatic invertebrates and fishes show positive shifts." It was a surprising and welcomed discovery. "So what does dam removal have to do with serendipity? Well . . ." wrote Dr. George, "just about everything."

You'd think this would end the story of the recovery of Jamawissa Creek, but removing the dam was only the first step in habitat restoration. One year after the barrier came down, Riverkeeper returned to the site. The stream had spent the year after the dam was removed reestablishing its pathway, but now came the next step in the recovery process.

Riverkeeper and its volunteers were ready. Armed with trees, shrubs, and shovels, they planted fifteen trees and forty-five shrubs supplied by the NYSDEC's Trees for Tribs program. Not only would the trees help heal

The blue crab, a crustacean found in the Hudson River, has ecological, recreational, and commercial importance.

the area disturbed by the construction equipment used to remove the dam, but the plants would also create shade to keep the stream water cool for fish to thrive as well as prevent erosion on the banks.

"We work for the creeks and the organisms that live here," said Dr. George, and he is going to keep on working for them through Riverkeeper.

5
PROTECTING THE RIVER'S FUTURE

All Riverkeeper projects strive to protect the Hudson River's future. Part of that work includes building future leaders who will carry the baton forward and looking for ways to ensure ongoing protections for the watershed. One of the successful collaborations began in 2020 in the riverside city of Troy, New York.

WATER JUSTICE LAB

The Water Justice Lab, created by Riverkeeper and Media Sanctuary, was launched in 2020. The collaboration established a water quality sampling lab as part of Media Sanctuary's focus on air, water, soil, and community health. The lab builds community awareness about water justice issues impacting the Hudson River watershed and the eastern bankside community of North Troy, New York.

Like many other areas of the Hudson, Troy was home to the Muh-he-ka-ne-ok, known to Europeans as the Mahican or Mohican Indian tribe, who were forcibly removed from their lands by European settlers. The first settlers were the Dutch, followed by the English. Troy, a manufacturing center at the meeting point of the Hudson and Mohawk Rivers, became one of the most prosperous American cities in the nineteenth and early twentieth centuries. But like many old industrial cities, Troy lost its manufacturing base. These days Troy faces its share of environmental and social justice challenges. The Water Justice Lab is charged with mentoring youth so they are better able to help their communities address some of those issues.

In 2021 three teen water justice fellows, ranging from thirteen to sixteen years old, completed a short film, *Home Along the Hudson*, and uploaded it to YouTube. Viewers can see Riverkeeper's Sebastian Pillitteri supervising water testing by the teen fellows by positioning their sampling bottle upstream to catch the water and then pulling it out to cap it. Just like the water samples that Captain John collects from the Riverkeeper boat, this simple procedure is vital to the health of the river and the community of North Troy.

Starting in 2022, the Water Justice Lab focused on an eight-week course, Source to Estuary: Water Justice Summer Camp. This isn't the sort of camp that includes late-night bonfires and outdoor games. Instead, a group of focused Troy teens spent their days collecting and processing water samples for Riverkeeper's Upper Hudson water quality monitoring project under the direction of Riverkeeper staff. But that's not all. The teens also created content for the *Hudson Mohawk Magazine* radio broadcast/podcast focused on water literacy, water civics, and other river projects. Between visits to tributaries and wastewater treatment sites and trips on the river on a solar pontoon boat, they also organized virtual meetups for environmental justice advocates focused on water issues. These teens contribute to Riverkeeper's hope for the future.

Water samples are gathered from the Upper Hudson River, between the Adirondack Mountains and Troy, by volunteers coordinated

Riverkeeper's community science coordinator, Sebastian Pillitteri, works with teen water justice fellow Henry Kimball to examine Hudson River water samples at the Nature Lab in Troy, New York.

by Riverkeeper. These samples are carefully kept on ice and in the dark—to avoid bacteria growth or die-off in transit—and then they are tested by the teens at the Media Sanctuary in North Troy. Mentored by Sebastian, the teens follow a series of steps, first pouring water into a mixing bottle, then adding a chemical reagent that aids in the detection of bacteria and shaking before placing the sample into a tray that has multiple wells that each hold sample water and reagent. The tray is sealed and put into an incubator, which is like a specially designed oven that can maintain specific temperatures for scientific experiments, just like Carol does on the boat. After twenty-four to twenty-eight hours at forty-one degrees Celsius, the samples are removed and examined. The water is tested for fecal indicator bacteria that could come from sewage. The number of wells that glow indicate the concentration of bacteria in the water at the time the sample was taken. Samples that cause multiple wells to glow have bacteria that could be harmful to swimmers. The results of all samples are recorded and posted at riverkeeper.org so that people who enjoy swimming and other recreation can make informed choices about when and where to enter the water. Looking at the data, the team can see firsthand the water quality in different river locations. "It didn't surprise me that the more polluted water was from the more urban areas. People don't realize how closely related the environment is with racial discrimination," said teen water justice fellow Genesis Cooper.

Nature Lab water justice fellow Henry Kimball collects a water sample at the Lansingburgh Boat Launch.

Building strong leaders, like those from the Water Justice Lab, is vital, but there are other ways to think about protecting the future of the river. Another way to ensure the safety of the river moving forward is to help the river advocate for itself.

RIGHTS FOR THE RIVER

Tracy Brown is always looking for ways that Riverkeeper can be a voice for the waterways and the voiceless, but we've seen how others are also looking out for the river. What if the river had the same legal rights as a person? Thomas Linzey, senior legal counsel for the Center for Democratic and Environmental Rights, is recognized as the founder of the rights of nature movement. He wrote the first rights of nature law. According to him, those rights would include the right to exist, to thrive, to regenerate, to evolve, to perform natural species or ecosystem functions, to be restored, to habitat, to clean water and to flow, and to a healthy environment and climate. Sounds like something that could really help the Hudson River in the future, doesn't it? The river would still need people to be involved with its health, but it could have legal standing and be viewed as more important than a commodity to be exploited by humans.

The Religious Organizations Along the River (ROAR) think the Hudson River deserves these rights, and they have joined their voices to work on behalf of the Hudson. All voices are necessary to keep our rivers vital and healthy.

As volunteers were cleaning up the banks during Sweep in May, the Sisters of Charity of New York, members of ROAR, were creating a video conversation to discuss the rights of rivers and, specifically, the rights of the Hudson River. These rights weren't a new idea. The rights of parts of the nonhuman natural world have already been declared in other countries and elsewhere in the United States. The Universal Declaration on the Rights of Rivers was signed by more than forty governments and two hundred organizations, as reported by the 2020 International Union for Conservation of Nature (IUCN) World Conservation Congress. The declaration states that rivers are living entities, entitled to fundamental rights and legal guardians. In some cases legal guardianship can be granted to Indigenous communities who have been unofficial guardians for years, or in other cases to states that will implement these rights. But creating that declaration doesn't guarantee the same rights in every country.

In 2017 New Zealand became the first country to grant a river national personhood rights. The Whanganui River is the second largest river in the country. It flows into the Tasman Sea at Whanganui on the North Island. The Maori, the Indigenous Polynesian people of New Zealand, fought for these protections for the river for one hundred sixty years. The Maori have a traditional saying: "I am the river, the river is me." When the personhood designation was made, it meant that harming the river would be as if the tribe was harmed. What does this mean to the river?

At this point in United States history, a distinction exists between the rights of humans and those of nature. The natural world is viewed as a resource by our current laws. For example, Ben Price, community organizer for the Community Environmental Legal Defense Fund (CELDF), pointed out in the discussion that "forests were lumbering in the making," meaning they exist as our resource and for the profit of humans. But he adds that nature should have the right to "replenish [itself] after a harm, and to be replenished by those who have harmed [it], to continue an interplay between species."

Currently, the regulations that are in place by government entities

The Nature Lab is filled with photos of water justice fellows and the Hudson River.

don't stop the river from being harmed; they regulate the amount of harm that is caused.

Captain John spoke up. "The notion that the river needs its own rights is obvious to me from my perspective."

If the river had personhood rights, it would mean that if it is harmed by pollution, it could sue the entity that hurts it. It also means that it can own property and enter into contracts. Captain John raised the alarm about a recent controversial project. A cable that could endanger Hudson River fish migration was going to be placed under the river for many miles. But, as Captain John pointed out, despite protests and objections from Riverkeeper and others, he was told that the international energy corporation that proposed this project could move forward because "fish don't vote." But imagine if the river did have a voice and could speak out for itself in court. The outcome might be much different, and healthier, for the river bioregion.

The same year New Zealand awarded rights to their river, the Indian state of Uttarakhanda recognized and gave personhood rights to two rivers, the Ganges and Yamuna. Two years later, Bangladesh went one step further when it became the first country to grant all its rivers the same legal status as humans in a court of law. Unfortunately, the decision in India was later revoked. However, many other rivers have gained this special status, including South America's Amazon River, which runs through many nations, and the Magpie River in Canada. Here in the United States, the Yurok Tribe has granted the Klamath River in Northern California personhood. It is the first river in the United States to gain this status, although its status is not yet recognized by federal law.

The Klamath River flows through the lands of the Yurok Tribe in California, but water management and climate change have challenged the water's path and the river's life-giving salmon population. Giving the river personhood rights means that the river has the right to exist, according to Amy Cordalis, general counsel for the Yurok Tribe. On May 9, 2019, the Yurok Tribal Council approved Resolution No. 19-40. It gave

A map of the Hudson River wraps around the door to the Nature Lab.

the river the right "to flourish and to naturally evolve and a right to a stable climate free from human-caused climate change impacts," quoted Amy from the resolution. The tribe and its members already had a strong relationship with the river, known to the tribe as "We-roy." Why grant these rights now? Much had to do with the change of societal values during our climate crisis, claimed Amy. She also acknowledged that New Zealand has led the way.

Also in North America, Ohio voters approved a 2019 measure, "Lake Erie Bill of Rights," to grant personhood to Lake Erie. Unfortunately, the measure was struck down by a federal judge in 2020. The fight to protect Lake Erie continues.

According to Nez Percé tribal member Elliott Moffett, the Nez Percé Tribal Council followed the Yurok example and passed a resolution in 2020 to recognize the Snake River as a living being. And as of 2023, three dozen municipalities and tribal governments have adopted rights of nature in the United States.

Will the Hudson River or any other waterways obtain this status in the future? And if so, will that status help restore the Hudson and other rivers to healthy ecosystems that survive in concert with the people on their shores? We can only hope. Meanwhile, the movement continues. Organizations like ROAR and other activists continue to push for personhood rights to protect our wild places. Enforcement of these rights will be as important as granting them.

WE ALL LIVE IN A WATERSHED

The Beatles may have thought that we all live in a yellow submarine, but in reality, we all live in a watershed. As Charles Kuralt wrote in *The Magic of Rivers*, "I started out thinking of America as highways and state lines. As I got to know it better, I began to think of it as rivers."

What if we all thought of America as rivers instead, as Charles Kuralt did? If Tracy Brown had her wish, our watersheds would play an even more prominent role in our lives, even in the form of our political districting. Imagine a world where we base much of our decision-making and voting on how effectively our representatives would safeguard our

Across from Nature Lab's water testing are the Waterford waters where John docked recently with Batu.

watersheds and how legislation would impact the vital resource of our water supply. Perhaps in the future, these crucial geographical areas will play such a role.

In the meantime, look at the highways we do have. Tracy Brown points out that many, such as the Saw Mill River Parkway and the Bronx River Parkway, are named after the rivers.

"So many people don't realize that those are all waterways; they just think of them as roads," said Tracy Brown. "And they have built the roads right on them too."

She adds that those roads, named after rivers, carry cars that pollute those very waterways. For example, salt used in the winter to de-ice the pavement eventually ends up in the waterways.

"We've made a lot of bad design choices. But, we're learning," said Tracy.

For now, we have to work together to raise awareness of the value of our watersheds. Our rivers need us as much as we need them. So, let's explore some simple ways that we can make a difference.

The *Clearwater* reminds each of us that we can make a difference on our own local river waters.

6

JOIN YOUR LOCAL RIVER TEAM

So many rivers across the United States now have Riverkeeper and Waterkeeper organizations that work day and night to protect them. Among them is the Snake River Waterkeeper organization, founded in Idaho in 2014. Modeled after the Hudson Riverkeeper, Snake River Waterkeeper fights for the health of the twisting, turning Pacific Northwest river by removing dams and calling out polluters that harm the ecosystem and its salmon and steelhead fish populations.

Colorado Riverkeeper John Weisheit is working with a broad group of activists to prevent damaging tar sands strip mining that will harm the Colorado River and its watershed. The river is facing record-low levels and further disruption to the ecosystem will impact the seven states where the river flows.

So many of these Riverkeeper organizations, like the Milwaukee Riverkeeper in Wisconsin and the Hudson Riverkeeper, sponsor spring river cleanups. All these organizations could use your help. Find out if your local river has an advocate organization or opportunities for you to join their events. See how you can get involved with them. Even if your river doesn't have a specific organization or Riverkeeper in charge, you can still protect and preserve your local river in many ways.

"People want to help," said Tracy. "People who are doing something else and don't have the luxury that I have, of doing this every day and focusing on what they care about the most every day, want to come home and give a few hours."

Like the adults who volunteer their time to Riverkeeper after work or on weekends, you can also lend a hand or a voice when you aren't in school.

Riverkeeper's patrol boat provides important data each year to help keep the river ecosystem healthy for everyone.

ANOTHER HUDSON PATROL

On a Monday morning in late August, Captain John, Carol, and Batu were back on the patrol boat for another voyage north on the Hudson River. The day was overcast and in the low seventies when they arrived at the dock in Hudson, New York. Rain was again in the forecast, but the morning was now clear and the water still.

After taking samples, the boat moved on to other monitoring sites. It sailed past numerous birds, including the osprey nest Captain John had witnessed, a bald eagle in a tree, and a double-crested cormorant perched on a buoy. The living river never disappoints anyone who takes the time to enjoy and study it. Life is everywhere.

The patrol boat docked for a short time to sample the water in one of the river's old landing towns, Coxsackie, New York, where visitors to Riverside Park could sit on benches engraved with Mohican quotes including: "When you go into the world take your whole self with you—your roots—and plant them in your new world."—Dorothy Davids, Mohican.

As Riverkeeper's patrol boat sails on, it joins with others to celebrate a landmark "Save the Hudson" bill to halt radioactive wastewater discharges in the river.

Riverside interpretive signs remind us of past industries—brick-making, ice-harvesting, shipbuilding, metalworking, and barrelmaking—that made these communities flourish but took their toll on the river's ecosystem and native people. Carved into the stone edging along the riverside park path are the words of Hudson Valley naturalist John Burroughs, which couldn't be more timely or urgent today as we work toward preserving our environment: "For anything worth having, one must pay the price; and the price is always work, patience, love, self-sacrifice."

The Hudson River will continue to impact our world. And Riverkeeper will help guide it into a cleaner, healthier future. While Captain John continued his August river journey, Riverkeeper president Tracy Brown joined others to celebrate the Congressional House passage of the NY-NJ Watershed Protection Act. Tracy called the Hudson "an ecological wonder and home to the most populous and economically significant region in the country." She continued praising the transformative act's progress

Inscribed benches like this one remind us of the people who stepped on this land before us.

and those pushing it forward, including Riverkeeper. It is "a recognition of the vibrant and dogged efforts of forward-thinking elected officials, local governments, and organizations who have fought to bring the Hudson back from the brink."

While this book and Captain John's summer river patrolling conclude, the story of the Hudson River and your river continues. "The story," wrote Thomas Berry in his book years ago, "as we have seen, is a poignant one, a story with its glory, but not without its tragedy."

You, the reader of this book, now have to decide how you can add to the story of the Hudson and other rivers across the globe.

AUTHOR'S NOTE

I grew up beside the Hudson River. Every day I walked to my school bus stop with a view of the river in front of me. As a teen, I moved to another house even closer to the river. It brought the river directly into view from my window. My first job, as a lifeguard, was at a riverside park in Haverstraw, New York. I picked up stones, polished glass, and shells from the river's shore; sailed on its waters; and went birding with my dad on its banks. Later, I went to a college on a hill beside the river and saw the sun's golden orange set across the shore every day. As an adult I moved north, where the river is narrower. I continue to bird on its banks, kayak its waters, visit its lighthouses, and hike on Hudson Valley trails. So many of us have similar experiences with a river. Our life flows along with the waters close to us.

This book was birthed out of the COVID-19 pandemic, a time when I wasn't traveling to faraway places for book research and was focused on the natural world around me. It's been a joy to work on as I rediscover my river and bring its story to my readers all around the world.

ACKNOWLEDGMENTS

My gratitude spills over the riverbanks for so many on this book. First and foremost, the wonderful staff at Riverkeeper: namely, Leah Rae, Tracy Brown, John Lipscomb, Carol Knudson, Sebastian Pillitteri, and Katie Leung. I loved my time with them on the river and on its banks! I couldn't have written this without them and their endless enthusiasm for the river and this project. I'd love to give a shout-out to the folks at Hudson Sloop Club—my fellow Sweep volunteers who shared trash bags and let me photograph them, including Adam Weinert, Kate Treacy, John Ganning, Stephanie Asqueri, and Sarah Dibben and her family. Thanks also to the fabulous crew at Holiday House Books. It was so much fun reconnecting with this great team, headed by Mary Cash. Many thanks to my critique buds, fellow nonfiction authors, including Anita Sanchez and Lois Huey.

GLOSSARY

algal bloom: A rapid increase in the amount of algae in fresh or salt water that can endanger people and wildlife.

bioregion: A region defined by ecological and geographic characteristics.

brackish: Water that is more salty than fresh, but less salty than the ocean.

catadromous: The term for a fish that migrates down a river to the sea to spawn.

chlorophyll: The pigment that makes plants green and helps plants absorb light to be converted into energy through photosynthesis. Increased levels in water can indicate an algal bloom.

creek: A stream, brook, or other minor tributary.

dam: A barrier to hold back water flow.

ecosystem: A biological community of organisms and their habitat.

estuary: The tidal mouth of a large river where the river meets the ocean.

flyway: A migration path used by birds.

headwaters: A tributary stream of a river close to or becoming the river's source.

kill: The Dutch word for *stream*.

latitude: The distance north or south of the equator.

longitude: The measurement east or west of the prime meridian.

nature-based infrastructure: A system where natural features are combined with engineering to modify an ecosystem that benefits people and nature.

PCB: An abbreviation for *polychlorinated biphenyls*, mixtures of harmful compounds used as coolants and lubricants in transformers, capacitors, and other electrical equipment.

pH scale: A measurement of a liquid's acidity or basicity.

pollution: The presence of a substance that is harmful.

precipitation: Water in different states falling from the sky as rain, sleet, snow, or hail.

river: A large flowing body of water that moves in a channel to a sea, lake, or other body of water.

Riverkeeper: The organization that works to maintain the health and well-being of the Hudson River.

salinity: The amount of dissolved salt in a water of body.

sediment: Solid materials, such as pieces of rocks, sticks, leaves, or other items, that settle on the bottom of a river. It can provide hiding and nesting areas for creatures but also make water cloudy.

sloop: A sailboat with one mast.

spawn: To deposit eggs.

tributary: A river or stream flowing into another river or lake.

turbidity: A measure of clarity (or clearness) of water.

water basin: A larger watershed that is made up of smaller watersheds. New York State has seventeen major water basins, including the Lower Hudson River and the Upper Hudson River.

watershed: An area of land where water collects and then flows into rivers, basins, or seas.

RESOURCES

GET INVOLVED

WHAT CAN YOU DO TO SAFEGUARD RIVERS AND WATERSHEDS NEAR YOU? HERE ARE A FEW IDEAS:

JOIN A RIVER CLEANUP

Find out about local river cleanup events. Wear old clothes and gloves to join in picking up trash on the banks of your local river or tributary. Every pair of hands helps support river health.

BE A WATER TESTER

Ask your local river organization if you can volunteer as a water tester. Riverkeeper's citizen science participation starts in April of each year. Limited spots for volunteers are available for a six-month commitment. Your local river might offer something similar.

PROTECT THE DRAIN

Use biodegradable soaps for cleaning clothes, the house, and yourself so that when those cleaners wash down the drain, they won't pollute your local waterway. Remember that whatever goes down your drain could end up in local streams, creeks, and rivers.

PLANT A TREE

Trees have roots that hold on to soil that could run into rivers and streams. Planting tree seedlings will one day help absorb pollutants in the air and combat climate change. And if you can't plant a tree, protect one. You'll be helping to curb climate change and prevent soil erosion.

BAN THE BUG SPRAY

Besides killing important pollinators, chemical pesticides can seep into the ground and pollute streams, tributaries, and rivers, as DDT did decades ago. Try a natural oil or spray bug repellent that won't pollute or harm wildlife but will keep you bite-free.

SPREAD THE NEWS

All rivers need people to speak up on their behalf. Be a voice for your river—link river information and articles to your social media. Talk to your friends or use school presentations as an opportunity to inform your classmates. Take photos of your river to add to your social media posts. Promote healthy river activities.

USE WATER WISELY

There are lots of ways you can conserve water at home. Use leftover water from a drinking glass or pet bowl to water a tree or house plant rather than pouring it down the drain. Take shorter showers. Don't run the faucet when you brush your teeth. There are lots of other ways if you look around. And all of them contribute to keeping your local waterways healthy.

DISCOVER THESE HUDSON RIVER PLACES

Bannerman Castle, Beacon, NY: bannermancastle.org

Hudson River Islands State Park, Coxsackie, NY: parks.ny.gov/parks/hudson riverislands/maps.aspx

Corning Preserve, Albany, NY: albany.org/listing/albany-corning-preserve -jennings-landing/159/

Little Island, New York City: littleisland.org

Hudson River Maritime Museum, Kingston, NY: hrmm.org (Take a solar boat tour!)

Hudson Highlands Nature Museum, Cornwall-on-Hudson, NY: hhnm.org

Hudson River Museum, Yonkers, NY: hrm.org

Hudson River Skywalk, Catskill, NY: hudsonriverskywalk.org

Walkway Over the Hudson, Poughkeepsie, NY: walkway.org

EXPLORE THESE WATERWAY ADVOCACY ORGANIZATIONS

American Rivers: americanrivers.org

Clearwater: clearwater.org

The Hudson River Estuary Program, NYS Dept of Environmental Conservation, Reg 3: dec.ny.gov/lands/4920.html

Hudson River Watershed Alliance: facebook.com/HudsonRiverWatershedAlliance/events/?ref=page_internal

National Wild and Scenic Rivers System: rivers.gov

Rights of Rivers: rightsofrivers.org/#declaration

ROAR: facebook.com/ROARHUDSON

The Sanctuary for Independent Media: mediasanctuary.org

Scenic Hudson: scenichudson.org

Sunrise Movement: sunrisemovement.org

Waterkeeper Alliance (Find your local Waterkeeper): waterkeeper.org

READ

Baron, Robert, and Thomas Locker. *Hudson: The Story of a River*. Golden, CO: Fulcrum Publishing, 2004.

Castaldo, Nancy F. *River Wild*. Chicago, IL: Chicago River Press, 2006.

Cherry, Lynne. *A River Ran Wild: An Environmental History*. New York, NY: Harcourt Brace/Gulliver Green, 1992.

Cooper, Elisha. *River*. New York, NY: Orchard Books, 2019.

Mehnert, Volker. *Great Rivers of the World*. Prestel Junior, 2021.

Newman, Patricia. *A River's Gifts: The Mighty Elwha River Reborn*. Minneapolis, MN: Millbrook Press, 2023.

Talbott, Hudson. *River of Dreams*. New York, NY: G. P. Putnam's Sons Books for Young Readers, 2009.

WATCH

Explore Riverkeeper Videos: youtube.com/user/hudsonriverkeeper.

Alewives in the Wynants Kill: youtube.com/watch?v=9Nj8HASjG3l&feature =youtu.be.

Alewives and the Concrete Channel of the Wynants Kill: youtube.com /watch?v=smDdKpiV-so.

Home Along the Hudson: youtu.be/oUP-9B2l1Il.

Seven Sentinels: Lighthouses of the Hudson River: youtu.be/zEFnBc4b5kc.

Hope on the Hudson: Undamming the Hudson River, Oceans 8 Films, Pro ducer and Director John Bowermaster, March 19, 2019, hudsonriverstories.com /undamming-the-hudson.

Hope on the Hudson: City on the Water. Riverkeeper, Oceans 8 Films, Producer and Director John Bowermaster, September 6, 2018, youtube.com /watch?v=1E7w-o1TUh4.

Hope on the Hudson 2: Restoring the Clearwater. Oceans 8 Films, Producer and Director John Bowermaster, March 6, 2018, vimeo.com/258875113.

CELEBRATE RIVERS ALL YEAR LONG

JANUARY

Eagle Days: Head to St. Louis for eagle watching on the Mississippi River. greatriversgreenway.org/eagledays.

APRIL

Family Canoe Trips: Explore the ecology of wetlands typically found around the Chesapeake Bay. Find out how wetlands help fish and crabs living in the Bay and how scientists study this type of ecosystem. Sponsored by the Smithsonian Environmental Research Center. serc.si.edu.

Mississippi Flyway Birding Festival: Join birders along the Mississippi Flyway for a celebration of the spring bird migration. There are seminars and activities to welcome the birds back to the region. mindfulbirding.org/festivals /checklist/54.

MAY

Holyoke Gas & Electric's Annual Shad Derby: Hadley Falls Dam, Holyoke, Massachusetts. Fish for shad at one of the world's premier fishing spots. Win prizes for your catch. Registration required. hged.com/community-environment /recreation/shad-derby.aspx.

Run with the Alewives: This is an annual Maine favorite for all ages. Learn all about this famous alewife run and its distinguished history. If the alewives cooperate, and they most always do, you will witness one of New England's most spectacular fish runs. damariscottamills.org/run-with-the-alewives.

Hudson River Sweep Annual Riverbank Cleanup: riverkeeper.org/news -events/events/rvk-events/10th-annual-riverkeeper-sweep.

Sail on the Tennessee River: Memorial Day through Labor Day sail aboard the *Southern Belle Riverboat*. It sails from Chattanooga, Tennessee. chattanooga riverboat.com.

JUNE

National Rivers Month: Visit your local river for lots of activities! Spread the word about river conservation.

Clearwater Festival: Annual festival with music in New York's Hudson Valley. clearwaterfestival.org.

JULY

Annual Tuber's Cruise on the James River: Float down the James River in an inner tube and enjoy the river up close and personal or ride in a batteau! jamesrivertour.com.

Annual Hudson River Paddle: Celebrate the Hudson River by kayak. Paddle from Albany south to Manhattan. hudsonrivervalley.org/paddle.

AUGUST

Annual Great Hudson River Estuary Fish Count: Join with naturalists on the river or shore to help collect data on the river's fish population using seine nets, minnow traps, or rods and reels. All the fish are released back into the water after they are identified and counted. dec.ny.gov/lands/97891.html.

OCTOBER

Annual Connecticut River Source to Sea Cleanup: This is a four-state river cleanup. Start a local group or check for cleanup sites near you. Sponsored by CT River Watershed Council. ctriver.org/our-work/source-to-sea -cleanup.

DECEMBER

Christmas Ship Parade: Annual parade of ships on the Columbia and Willamette Rivers. The Christmas Ship Fleet averages about fifty-five to sixty boats between the two fleets. Both fleets will be out every night for two weeks in December. christmasships.org/schedule/columbia-river.

HUDSON RIVER TIMELINE

Like we say the wheels of justice grind slowly, you'll see that many of these cases have also moved slowly, some over decades. But the river is ancient, and it isn't going anywhere. As long as we all continue to advocate for it, we will see successes.

15,000 years ago: Glaciers stretched out throughout the region during the Great Ice Age. As they melted, they carved out a channel that became the Hudson River.

7,000 years ago (Neolithic Period): First people live in what is now Westchester County.

Around 500 CE (Late Woodland Period): Lenape inhabit the Hudson Valley.

1400s–1600s: The Lenape establish the Hudson waterfront area, now known as Greenwich Village.

1524: Giovanni da Verrazano explores the "Narrows" and becomes the first European to visit New York Bay.

1609: Henry Hudson sails up the river under the Dutch flag.

1626: The Munsee tribe "sells" the island of Manhattan to Peter Stuyvesant.

1775: A log boom and chain is stretched across the river to block the English during the Revolutionary War.

1807: Robert Fulton's steamship, the *North River Steamboat*, launches its maiden voyage from Pier 45 in Manhattan. It reaches Albany in thirty-two hours.

1825: The Erie Canal is completed, joining the Hudson River with Lake Erie.

1890s: A group of women activists led by Cecilia Gaines and Elizabeth Vermilye lead the preservation of the Palisade cliffs of the Lower Hudson River.

1899: Refuse Act forbids pollution of national waterways and awards a bounty for turning in polluters.

1927: The Holland Tunnel opens for traffic.

1929: PCBs are first made by Monsanto Company.

1947–1977: General Electric (GE) uses polychlorinated biphenyls (PCBs).

1956: Construction begins on the Indian Point Nuclear Power Plant in Buchanan, New York.

1963: Consolidated Edison applies for a license to build a huge hydroelectric power facility on Storm King Mountain. It's approved in 1965.

1965: Robert Boyle testifies against the Storm King hydroelectric project.

1966: Hudson River Fisherman's Association (HRFA) is established.

1966: Pete Seeger builds the *Clearwater* sloop.

1968: HRFA sues Penn Central Railroad for releasing oil into the Croton River, using the Refuse Act of 1899, and wins $2,000.

1969: The *Clearwater* is launched.

1970: First Earth Day.

1972: Clean Water Act passed.

1975: The Fort Edward Dam is removed by Niagara Mohawk Power Company, releasing PCBs downstream and turning the Hudson River into the largest Superfund site in America.

1975: PCBs are found in Hudson River fish, and enforcement begins against General Electric. GE must create a $7 million cleanup fund, build pollution stoppage facilities, and stop using PCBs by 1977.

1977: The production of PCBs is stopped, and GE discontinues use.

1980: Con Edison abandons plans for a hydroplant on Storm King.

1984: Robert F. Kennedy Jr. becomes Riverkeeper's Chief Prosecuting Attorney, and HRFA announces plans to sue Exxon for discharging polluted salt water in the Hudson from tankers.

1986: HRFA and Riverkeeper merge under the Riverkeeper name.

1992: The National Alliance of River, Sound, and Baykeepers, based on the Riverkeeper model, is founded.

1997: Riverkeeper helps negotiate and signs the Watershed Memorandum Agreement, forming the cooperation of New York City and upstate watershed communities to provide water protection

1999: Waterkeeper Alliance, formerly the National Alliance of River, Sound, and Baykeepers, is established with Kennedy at its head. There are now thirty Keeper groups worldwide.

2000: John Lipscomb becomes Riverkeeper's first boat captain and provides a full-time presence on the Hudson River aboard the *R. Ian Fletcher*.

2001: Riverkeeper begins to campaign for the closure of the Indian Point Nuclear Power Plant.

2003: Riverkeeper persuades the U.S. Environmental Protection Agency (EPA) to establish a 153-mile "no discharge" zone in the Hudson to prevent boats from releasing sewage in the river.

2004: Riverkeeper and residents from Greenpoint, Brooklyn, sue ExxonMobil for the more than seventeen million gallons of oil leaking from their facilities, which is in violation of the Clean Water Act and Resource Conservation and Recovery Act.

2006–2008: Riverkeeper's water quality monitoring studies begin.

2007: NYS attorney general Andrew Cuomo files suit against ExxonMobil to force the oil spill cleanup in Greenpoint.

2008: First water quality test results are posted.

2010: After six years, a settlement between Exxon and New York State is met that requires full cleanup of the Brooklyn site. Greenpoint residents receive a $19.5 million environmental benefit plan.

2010: EPA orders GE to remedy the river's PCB contamination.

2012: Riverkeeper helps get Endangered Species Act protections for Atlantic sturgeon, establishes new fishing regulations for river herring, and completes an American shad study.

2015: Riverkeeper helps Rockland County residents defeat desalination plant development to supply drinking water. A new plan is created based on conservation.

2016: Riverkeeper, New York State Energy Research Development Authority (NYSERDA), and Entergy complete an agreement to close Indian Point by 2021 and speed up decommissioning of the harmful nuclear power plant.

2016: An obsolete dam on Wynants Kill is identified and removed to help restore a migration path for Hudson fish.

2017: Riverkeeper builds community efforts to end the Coast Guard's project to build forty-three new anchorage berths for commercial vessels on the Hudson.

2019: Hudson River named one of the nation's "Most Endangered Rivers."

2021: Tracy Brown becomes president and Hudson Riverkeeper.

2022: One million acres of freshwater wetlands are protected by new New York State law.

EXPLORE NORTH AMERICA'S THREE MILLION MILES OF RIVERS

UNITED STATES

ALABAMA
Alabama River
Black Warrior River
Cahaba River
Chattahoochee River
Conecuh River
Coosa River
Elk River
Tallapoosa River
Tennessee River
Tombigbee River

ALASKA
Chuitna River
Colville River
Copper River
Kobuk River
Koyukuk River
Kuskokwim River
Noatak River
Susitna River
Tanana River
Yukon River

ARIZONA
Colorado River
Gila River
Salt River
Verde River

ARKANSAS
Arkansas River
Bayou Bartholomew
Ouachita River
Red River
Saint Frances River
White River

CALIFORNIA
Colorado River
Klamath River
San Joaquin River
Sacrament River

COLORADO

Arkansas River

Canadian River

Cimmarron River

Colorado River

Green River

North Platte River

Rio Grande

Smoky Hill River

CONNECTICUT

Connecticut River

Housatonic River

DELAWARE

Delaware River

DISTRICT OF COLUMBIA

Anacostia River

Potomac River

FLORIDA

Apalachicola River

Chattahoochee River

Saint John's River

GEORGIA

Chattahoochee River

Flint River

Ogeechee River

Savannah River

HAWAII

Hanalei River

Wailuku River

IDAHO

Bear River

Clark Fork

Kootenai River

Owyhee River

Salmon River

Snake River

ILLINOIS

Illinois River

Kaskaskia River

Mississippi River

Ohio River

Rock River

Wabash River

INDIANA

Ohio River

St. Joseph River

Wabash River

White River

IOWA

Big Sioux River

Cedar River

Des Moines River

Iowa River

Mississippi River

Missouri River

KANSAS

Arkansas River

Cimarron River

Kansas River

Missouri River

Neosho River

Republican River

Smoky Hill River

KENTUCKY

Cumberland River

Green River

Licking River

Mississippi River

Ohio River

Tennessee River

LOUISIANA

Bayou Bartholomew

Mississippi River

Ouachita River

Pearl River

Red River

Sabine River

MAINE

Androscoggin River

Kennebec River

Saint John River

MARYLAND

Potomac River

Susquehanna River

MASSACHUSETTS

Charles River

Merrimack River

MICHIGAN

Grand River

Muskegon River

Saint Lawrence River

MINNESOTA

Cedar River

Des Moines River

Minnesota River

Mississippi River

Red River

Saint Lawrence River

Wapsipinicon River

MISSISSIPPI

Big Black River

Mississippi River

Pearl River

Tennessee River

MISSOURI

Des Moines River

Mississippi River

Missouri River

Saint Frances River

White River

MONTANA

Bighorn River
Clark Fork
Kootenai River
Milk River
Missouri River
Musselshell River
Powder River
Yellowstone River

NEBRASKA

Big Blue River
Missouri River
Niobrara River
North Platte River
Platte River
Republican River
White River

NEVADA

Colorado River
Humboldt River
Owyhee River

NEW HAMPSHIRE

Androscoggin River
Connecticut River

NEW JERSEY

Delaware River
Hudson River

NEW MEXICO

Canadian River
Cimarron River
Gila River
Pecos River
Rio Grande
San Juan River

NEW YORK

Allegheny River
Delaware River
Hudson River
Saint Lawrence River
Susquehanna River

NORTH CAROLINA

New River
Roanoke River

NORTH DAKOTA

James River
Little Missouri River
Missouri River
Pembina River
Red River
Sheyenne River
Yellowstone River

OHIO

Ohio River
Scioto River
Wabash River

OKLAHOMA
Arkansas River
Canadian River
Cimarron River
Neosho River
North Canadian River
Red River
Verdigris River

OREGON
Columbia River
Owyhee River
Snake River

PENNSYLVANIA
Allegheny River
Delaware River
Susquehanna River

RHODE ISLAND
Blackstone River
Maumee River

SOUTH CAROLINA
Catawba River
Edisto River
Pee Dee River
Savannah River

SOUTH DAKOTA
Big Sioux River
James River
Little Missouri River
Missouri River
White River

TENNESSEE
Clinch River
Cumberland River
Harpeth River
Mississippi River
Tennessee River

TEXAS
Brazos River
Canadian River
Colorado River
Neches River
Nueces River
Pecos River
Red River
Rio Grande
Sabine River
Trinity River

UTAH
Colorado River
Green River
San Juan River

VERMONT
Connecticut River

Otter Creek

VIRGINIA
Clinch River

James River

New River

Potomac River

Roanoke River

WASHINGTON
Columbia River

Elwha River

Snake River

WEST VIRGINIA
New River

Ohio River

Potomac River

WISCONSIN
Mississippi River

Rock River

Saint Lawrence River

Wisconsin River

WYOMING
Green River

Little Missouri River

Niobrara River

North Platte River

Powder River

Snake River

Wind River

Yellowstone River

CANADA

ALBERTA
Liard River

Milk River

North Saskatchewan River

Saskatchewan River

South Saskatchewan River

Slave River

BRITISH COLUMBIA
Columbia River

Fraser River

Yukon River

MANITOBA
Athabasca River

Nelson River

Saskatchewan River

NEW BRUNSWICK
Saint John River

NEWFOUNDLAND AND LABRADOR
Churchill River

NORTHWEST TERRITORIES
Liard River
Slave River
Mackenzie River

NOVA SCOTIA
Saint Mary's River

NUNAVUT
Coppermine River

ONTARIO
Albany River
Ottawa River
Saint Lawrence River

PRINCE EDWARD ISLAND
Hillsborough River

QUEBEC
Le Grande River
Ottawa River
Saint Lawrence River

SASKATCHEWAN
North Saskatchewan River
Saskatchewan River
South Saskatchewan River

YUKON
Liard River
Yukon River

MEXICO

Balsas River
Colorado River
Culiacán River
Grijalva–Usumacinta Rivers
Lerma River
Nazas–Aguanaval Rivers
Rio Grande

RIVERKEEPERS AND OTHER WATERKEEPER ORGANIZATIONS

UNITED STATES

ALABAMA

Alabama Rivers Alliance
alabamarivers.org

Black Warrior Riverkeeper
blackwarriorriver.org

Cahaba Riverkeeper
cahabariverkeeper.org

Choctawhatchee Riverkeeper
choctawhatcheeriver.org

Coosa Riverkeeper
coosariver.org

Hurricane Creekkeeper
yourcreekkeeper.blogspot.com

Little River Waterkeeper
alabamarivers.org/our
-partners/one-world-adventure
-company-little-river-waterkeeper/

Mobile Baykeeper
mobilebaykeeper.org

Tennessee Riverkeeper
tennesseeriverkeeper.org

Waterkeepers Alabama
waterkeepersalabama.org

ALASKA

Cook Inletkeeper
inletkeeper.org

ARIZONA

Black Mesa Waterkeeper
blackmesatrust.org

Friends of the Santa Cruz River
friendsofsantacruzriver.org

ARKANSAS

Arkansas Ozark Waterkeeper
arkansasozarkswaterkeeper.org

CALIFORNIA

California Coastkeeper Alliance
cacoastkeeper.org

Humboldt Baykeeper
humboldtbaykeeper.org

Inland Empire Waterkeeper
iewaterkeeper.org

Los Angeles Waterkeeper
lawaterkeeper.org

Monterey Waterkeeper
montereywaterkeeper.org

Orange County Coastkeeper
coastkeeper.org

Russian Riverkeeper
russianriverkeeper.org

San Diego Coastkeeper
sdcoastkeeper.org

San Luis Obispo Coastkeeper
bluefront.org/blue
movement/san-luis-obispo-slo
-coastkeeper/

Santa Barbara Channelkeeper
sbck.org

Ventura Coastkeeper
wishtoyo.org

Yuba River Waterkeeper
yubariver.org/advocate/

Klamath Riverkeeper
twitter.com/klamathriver?lang=en
facebook.com/klamathriverkeeper

COLORADO

Alamosa River
alamosariverfoundation.com

Animas Riverkeeper
sanjuancitizens.org/animas-river

Poudre Waterkeeper
savethepoudre.org

South Platte River Waterkeeper
denverwaterkeeper.org

Upper Colorado River Watershed
    Group
ucrwg.org

CONNECTICUT

Long Island Soundkeeper
savethesound.org

DELAWARE

Delaware Riverkeeper Network
delawareriverkeeper.org

DISTRICT OF COLUMBIA

Anacostia Riverkeeper
anacostiariverkeeper.org

Potomac Riverkeeper
potomacriverkeeper.org

FLORIDA

Apalachicola Bay & Riverkeeper
apalachicolariverkeeper.org

Calusa Waterkeeper
calusawaterkeeper.org

Collier County Waterkeeper
colliercountywaterkeeper.org

Emerald Coastkeeper
emeraldcoastkeeper.org

Indian Riverkeeper
theindianriverkeeper.org

Kissimmee Waterkeeper
kissimmeewaterkeeper.org

Matanzas Riverkeeper
matanzasriverkeeper.org

Peace+Myakka Waterkeeper
peacemyakkawaterkeeper.org

Suncoast Waterkeeper
suncoastwater keeper.org

St. Johns Riverkeeper
stjohnsriverkeeper.org

Tampa Bay Waterkeeper
tampabaywaterkeeper.org

GEORGIA

Altamaha Riverkeeper
altamahariverkeeper.org

Chattahoochee Riverkeeper
chattahoochee.org

Flint Riverkeeper
flintriverkeeper.org

Savannah Riverkeeper
savannahriverkeeper.org

Suwannee Riverkeeper
wwals.net

Upper Coosa Riverkeeper
coosa.org

HAWAII
Waiwai Ola Waterkeepers
    Hawaiian Islands
waterkeepershi.org

IDAHO
Lake Coeur d'Alene Waterkeeper
kealliance.org/water

Snake River Waterkeeper
snakeriverwaterkeeper.org

ILLINOIS
Wabash Riverkeeper
banksofthewabash.net
/wabash-riverkeeper

INDIANA
Wabash Riverkeeper
facebook.com/wabashriverkeeper/

IOWA
Iowa Rivers Revival
iowarivers.org/

KANSAS
Kansas Riverkeeper
kansasriver.org

KENTUCKY
Kentucky Riverkeeper
kyriverkeeper.org

LOUISIANA
Atchafalaya Basinkeeper
basinkeeper.org

Louisiana Bayoukeeper
facebook.com/Louisiana
BayouKeeper

Lower Mississippi Riverkeeper
bluefront.org/bluemovement
/lower-mississippi-riverkeeper/

MAINE
Casco Baykeeper
cascobay.org

MARYLAND
Assateague Coastkeeper
actforbays.org

Baltimore Harbor Waterkeeper
bluewaterbaltimore.org
/baltimore-harbor-waterkeeper

Chester Riverkeeper
shorerivers.org/chester

Choptank Riverkeeper
shorerivers.org/choptank

Gunpowder Riverkeeper
gunpowderriverkeeper.org

Miles-Wye Riverkeeper
shorerivers.org/miles-wye

Patuxent Riverkeeper
paxriverkeeper.org

Severn Riverkeeper
severnriverkeeper.org

Upper Potomac Riverkeeper
potomacriverkeeper.org

South & West/Rhode Riverkeeper,
 Inc.
arundelrivers.org

MASSACHUSETTS
Buzzards Baykeeper
savebuzzardsbay.org

Housatonic Riverkeeper
cleanthehousatonic.com

Nantucket Waterkeeper
nantucketlandcouncil.org
/water-protection/nantucket
-waterkeeper/

MICHIGAN
Detroit Riverkeeper
detroitriver.org

Grand Traverse Baykeeper
gtbay.org

St. Clair Channelkeeper
mrwa.org

Tip of the Mitt Waterkeeper
watershedcouncil.org

Yellow Dog Riverkeeper
yellowdogwatershed.org
/yellow-dog-riverkeeper/

MINNESOTA
Northeast Riverkeepers
 Fargo-Moorhead
riverkeepers.org

MISSISSIPPI
Pearl Riverkeeper
pearlriverkeeper.com

MISSOURI
Missouri Confluence Waterkeeper
missouriconfluencewaterkeeper.org

MONTANA
Big Blackfoot Riverkeeper
bigblackfootriverkeeper.org

Bitterroot River Protection
 Association
bitterrootriver.org

Upper Missouri Waterkeeper
uppermissouriwaterkeeper.org

NEBRASKA
Lower Platte River Corridor
    Alliance
lowerplatte.org/

NEVADA
Great Basin Waterkeeper
greatbasinwater.org
/who-we-are/great-basin-water
keeper/

Las Vegas Water Defender, a
    Colorado Riverkeeper Affiliate
lvwaterdefender.com

NEW HAMPSHIRE
Great Bay Piscataqua Waterkeeper
clf.org/making-an-impact/great
-bay-piscataqua-waterkeeper/

NEW JERSEY
Great Swamp Watershed Assoc.,
    a Passaic River Waterkeeper
    Alliance Affiliate
greatswamp.org

Hackensack Riverkeeper
hackensackriverkeeper.org

New York/New Jersey Baykeeper
nynjbaykeeper.org

Raritan Riverkeeper
nynjbaykeeper.org/resources
.programs/raritan.riverkeeper

NEW MEXICO
Rio Grande Waterkeeper
riograndewaterkeeper.org

NEW YORK
Buffalo Niagara Riverkeeper
bnwaterkeeper.org

Hudson Riverkeeper
riverkeeper.org

Lake George Waterkeeper
lakegeorgewaterkeeper.org

Peconic Baykeeper
peconicbaykeeper.org

Seneca Lake Guardian
senecalakeguardian.org

Upper St. Lawrence Riverkeeper
savetheriver.org/about-us
/riverkeeper/

NORTH CAROLINA
Broad Riverkeeper
mountaintrue.org/waters/broad
-riverkeeper

Cape Fear Riverkeeper
capefearriverwatch.org

Catawba Riverkeeper
catawbariverkeeper.org

Dan Riverkeeper
danriverkeeper.org

French Broad Riverkeeper
mountaintrue.org/waters
/french-broad-riverkeeper/

Upper Neuse Riverkeeper
neuseriver.org

Watauga Riverkeeper
mountaintrue.org/waters
/watauga-riverkeeper

Yadkin Riverkeeper
yadkinriverkeeper.org

NORTH DAKOTA
River Keepers of Fargo-Moorhead
fargomoorhead.org/what-to-do
/river-keepers

OHIO
Lake Erie Waterkeeper
lakeeriewaterkeeper.org

OKLAHOMA
Grand Riverkeeper LEAD
  Agency, Inc.
leadagency.org

OREGON
Columbia Riverkeeper
columbiariverkeeper.org

Rogue Riverkeeper
rogueriverkeeper.org

Tualatin Riverkeepers
tualatinriverkeepers.org

Willamette Riverkeeper
willamette-riverkeeper.org

PENNSYLVANIA
Delaware Riverkeeper
delawareriverkeeper.org

Lower Susquehanna Riverkeeper
lowersusquehannariverkeeper.org

Middle Susquehanna Riverkeeper
middlesusquehannariverkeeper.org/

Youghiogheny Riverkeeper
mtwatershed.com

RHODE ISLAND
Narragansett Baykeeper
savebay.org

SOUTH CAROLINA
Charleston Waterkeeper
charlestonwaterkeeper.org

Congaree Riverkeeper
congareeriverkeeper.org

Edisto Riverkeeper
edistofriends.org

Lumber Riverkeeper
facebook.com/lumberriverkeeper/

TENNESSEE
Tennessee Riverkeeper
tennesseeriverkeeper.org

TEXAS
Bayou City Waterkeeper
bayoucitywaterkeeper.org

Box and Stewardship Household
environmental-stewardship.org

San Antonio Bay Waterkeeper
nomorenurdles.org

UTAH
Colorado Riverkeeper
livingrivers.org

VERMONT
Lake Champlain Lakekeeper
clf.org/making-an-impact
/lake-champlain-lakekeeper

VIRGINIA
James Riverkeeper
jrava.org

Shenandoah Riverkeeper
shenandoahriverkeeper.org

WASHINGTON
Deschutes Estuary Restoration
deschutesestuary.org

North Sound Waterkeeper
re-sources.org/initiative/water
keeper

Puget Soundkeeper
pugetsoundkeeper.org

Spokane Riverkeeper
spokaneriverkeeper.org

Twin Harbors Waterkeeper
waterkeeper.org/news/author
/twin-harbors-waterkeeper/

WEST VIRGINIA

West Virginia Headwaters
   Waterkeeper
wvrivers.org

WISCONSIN

Milwaukee Riverkeeper
milwaukeeriverkeeper.org

WYOMING

Upper Green River Network
greenrivernetwork.org

INTERNATIONAL

AUSTRALIA

Yarra Riverkeeper
yarrariver.org.au

BAHAMAS

Waterkeepers Bahamas
waterkeepersbahamas.com

CANADA

Canadian Detroit Riverkeeper
detroitriver.org/riverkeeper

Fraser Riverkeeper
www.fraserriverkeeper.ca

Fundy Baykeeper, Conservation
   Council of New Brunswick
conservationcouncil.ca/fundy
-baykeeper/

Georgian Baykeeper
georgianbayforever.org

Grand Riverkeeper Labrador
grandriverkeeperlabrador.ca

Lake Ontario Waterkeeper
waterkeeper.ca

Ottawa Riverkeeper
ottawariverkeeper.ca

Moose Riverkeeper
mooseriverkeeper.wordpress.com

North Saskatchewan Riverkeeper
saskriverkeeper.ca

Petitcodiac Riverkeeper
petitcodiac.org

CHINA

Upper Yellow River Waterkeeper
gcbcn.org

IRAQ

Waterkeepers Iraq
waterkeepersiraq.org

IRELAND
Cork Harbour Waterkeeper
theswimguide.org/cork-harbour
-waterkeeper/

MEXICO
La Paz Waterkeeper
roclapaz.org

PERU
Amazonas Peru Waterkeeper
facebook.com/PERUDAR

RUSSIA
Guardians of River Hlynovka

SRI LANKA
Mahaweli River Waterkeeper
slwcs.org/mahaweli-waterkeeper

SWEDEN
Swedish Baltic Rivers Waterkeeper
ostersjolaxalvar.se

UNITED KINGDOM
London Waterkeeper
londonwaterkeeper.org.uk

BIBLIOGRAPHY

Adams, Arthur, G. editor. *The Hudson River in Literature*. New York: State University of New York Press, 1980.

Adams, Arthur G. *The Hudson River Guidebook*. New York: Fordham University Press, 1996.

Berry, Thomas. *The Dream of the Earth*. San Francisco: Sierra Club Books, 1988.

Boyle, Robert H. *The Hudson River*. New York: W. W. Norton, 1969.

Castaldo, Nancy. *River Wild: An Activity Guide to North American Rivers*. Chicago: Chicago Review Press, 2006.

Heraclitus. *The Fragments of the Work of Heraclitus of Ephesus on Nature*; Translated by G.T. Patrick. Baltimore: N. Murray, 1889.

Jacobs, Jane. *The Death and Life of Great American Cities*. New York: Modern Library, 2011.

Kuralt, Charles. *A Life on the Road*. New York: Ballantine Books, 1995.

Riverkeeper. *2022-2023 Impact Report*, Riverkeeper, 2023.

Rockwell, Rev. Charles. *The Catskill Mountains and the Region Around*. New York: Taintor Brothers & Co., 1869. catskillarchive.com/rockwell/index.htm

SOURCE NOTES

FRONT MATTER

p. *iii* "Friends . . . Hudson's wave.": http://www.catskillarchive.com/rockwell/14.htm

p. *iii* "You could . . . to you.": https://ia600203.us.archive.org/31/items/thefragmentsofth00herauoft/thefragmentsofth00herauoft.pdf

p. *vii* "Tell me a story . . . finfish,": Berry, p. 171

p. *vii* "a story . . . valley.": Ibid., p. 171

CHAPTER 1

p. 11 ". . . up the Hudson . . . Hudson.": Jacobs, p. 446

p. 12 "Coastal waters . . . feed on.": Boyle, Robert. *Sports Illustrated*, Oct. 26, 1970, Vol 33, No 17. p. 70.

p. 12 "It is also . . . kill people.": Ibid.

p. 13 "Sailing down . . . clear . . .": Seeger, Pete, https://www.youtube.com/watch?v=FzyYCuY161E&t=4s

p. 16 "clean renewable . . . infrastructure.": Author interview with Tracy Brown, July 25, 2022

p. 17 "fishable, swimmable and drinkable": Clean Water Act, Riverkeeper. https://www.riverkeeper.org/blogs/water-quality-blogs/after-50-years-of-the-clean-water-act-is-the-hudson-swimmable/.

CHAPTER 2

p. 21 "I was eight . . . safe?' ": Lindner, Elsbeth. "From Swimming in the River to Keeping It Clean," *River Journal Online News*, 11 Nov. 2021, https://riverjournalonline.com/around-town/for-the-local-good/from-swimming-in-the-river-to-keeping-it-clean/27649/

p. 21 "There's nothing . . . heart is,": Author interview with Tracy Brown, July 25, 2022

p. 22 "Living waterways . . . concern.": Author interview with Tracy Brown, July 25, 2022

p. 22 "People really . . . it,": Author interview with Tracy Brown, July 25, 2022

p. 22 "And when . . . that.": Author interview with Tracy Brown, July 25, 2022

p. 24   "Water is life-giving . . . life-taking.": Author interview with Tracy Brown, July 25, 2022

p. 27   "How do I . . . can be?": Author interview with Tracy Brown, July 25, 2022

CHAPTER 3

p. 29   "When I get . . . the fun.": Author interview with John Lipscomb, July 19, 2022

p. 30   "Feeling the walls . . . on me,": Author interview with Carol Knudson, August 22, 2022

p. 32   "peeking . . . a window": Author interview with John Lipscomb, August 22, 2022

p. 32   "It's a turbid . . . sediment.": Author interview with Carol Knudson, August 22, 2022

p. 36   "any river . . . itself.": Author interview with John Lipscomb, July 19, 2022

p. 38   "come up . . . home.": Bowermaster, Jon, director. "Undamming the Hudson." YouTube, Ocean 8 Films, 19 Mar., 2019. https://www.youtube.com/watch?v=Sg2wxsYtzOs

p. 39   "We're very . . . in return,": "Herring return to Wynants Kill after 85 years." *Riverkeeper*, 25 Aug. 2020. https://

www.riverkeeper.org/blogs/ecology/herring-return-wynants-kill-85-years/

p. 39   "It's a wondrous . . . that.": Bowermaster, Jon, director. "Undamming the Hudson." YouTube, Ocean 8 Films, 19, Mar., 2019. https://www.youtube.com/watch?v=Sg2wxsYtzOs

p. 39   "Success . . . last step.": Author interview with John Lipscomb, July 19, 2022

p. 41   "The river . . . help].": Author interview with John Lipscomb, July 19, 2022

pp. 41–42   "As you . . . leave it,": Author interview with John Lipscomb, July 19, 2022

p. 42   "passage-making": Author interview with John Lipscomb, July 19, 2022

p. 42   "The river can't say anything,": Author interview with John Lipscomb, July 19, 2022

CHAPTER 4

p. 47   "One Bag Challenges": Author interview with Katie Leung, August 9, 2022

p. 48   "We are trying . . . the Hudson." Author interview with Katie Leung, August 9, 2022

p. 51   "We now consider . . . removal,": Jackman, Dr. George. *The Three Princes of Dam Removal*, Water Resources Impact, American Water Resources Association, May/June 2022, p. 4, Vol. 24, No 3. https://online.flipping-book.com/view/997624649/

p. 51   "There is . . . Wall,": Jackman, Dr. George. "Habitat Restoration Along the Hudson – Riverkeeper," YouTube, hudsonriverkeeper, 4 Oct., 2021. https://www.youtube.com/watch?v=toQgUnyEU6U&t=42s

p. 51   "nature quickly . . . shifts.": Ibid.

p. 51   "So what . . . everything.": Ibid.

p. 52   "We work . . . here,": Ibid.

CHAPTER 5

p. 56   "It didn't surprise . . . discrimination,": "Home Along the Hudson." YouTube, mediasanctuary, 29 June, 2021. https://youtu.be/oUP-9B2l1lI?si=9w_pR6o3lbNjFUCf, Produced by The Sanctuary for Independent Media, 11 June, 2021.

p. 58   "I am the river . . . me.": https://www.bbc.com/travel/article/20200319-the-new-zealand-river-that-became-a-legal-person

p. 58   "forests were . . . making,": Price, Ben. "ROAR Rights of River 5.05.22," Vimeo, Sisters of Charity of New York, 6 May, 2022. https://vimeo.com/706973894

p. 58   "replenish . . . species.": "ROAR Rights of River 5.05.22," Vimeo, Sisters of Charity of New York, 6 May, 2022. https://vimeo.com/706973894

p. 60   "The notion . . . perspective.": Author interview with John Lipscomb, July 19, 2022

p. 61   "to flourish . . . impacts,": Cordalis, Amy. "Tribe Gives Personhood to Klamath River," NPR, Sept. 29, 2019. https://www.npr.org/2019/09/29/765480451/tribe-gives-personhood-to-klamath-river

p. 62   "Lake Erie Bill of Rights,": https://www.beyondpesticides.org/assets/media/documents/LakeErieBillofRights.pdf

p. 62   "I started out . . . rivers.": Kuralt, p. 159

p. 64   "So many . . . them too": Author interview with Tracy Brown, July 25, 2022

p. 64   "We've made . . . learning,": Author interview with Tracy Brown, July 25, 2022

CHAPTER 6

p. 67   "People want . . . hours.": Author interview with Tracy Brown, July 25, 2022

p. 68   "When you go . . . world.": Dorothy Davids, Mohican, engraved on Riverside Park bench, Coxsackie

p. 69 "For anything . . . self-sacrifice.": John Burroughs, Riverside Park path engraving

p. 69 "an ecological . . . country.":

Riverkeeper Instagram, August 25, 2022

p. 70 "a recognition . . . brink.": Author interview with Tracy, July 25, 2022

p. 70 "The story . . . tragedy. ": Berry, p. 171

PICTURE CREDITS

Photo courtesy of John P. Christin: p. 13

Picture courtesy of The Library of Congress: p. 10

Pictures courtesy of New York Public Library: pp. 6, 7

Map courtesy of New York State Department of Environmental Conservation: p. xii

Photos courtesy of Riverkeeper: pp. 28, 38, 40

All other photos were taken by the author.

INDEX

Italic page numbers refer to illustrations.